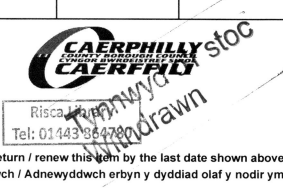

THE HOLY TERRORS

Also by Simon R. Green

The Ishmael Jones mysteries

THE DARK SIDE OF THE ROAD
DEAD MAN WALKING
VERY IMPORTANT CORPSES
DEATH SHALL COME
INTO THE THINNEST OF AIR
MURDER IN THE DARK *
TILL SUDDEN DEATH DO US PART *
NIGHT TRAIN TO MURDER *
THE HOUSE ON WIDOWS HILL *
BURIED MEMORIES *

The Gideon Sable series

THE BEST THING YOU CAN STEAL *
A MATTER OF DEATH AND LIFE *
WHAT SONG THE SIRENS SANG *
NOT OF THIS WORLD *

The Secret History series

PROPERTY OF A LADY FAIRE
FROM A DROOD TO A KILL
DR DOA
MOONBREAKER
NIGHT FALL

The Nightside series

JUST ANOTHER JUDGEMENT DAY
THE GOOD, THE BAD, AND THE UNCANNY
A HARD DAY'S KNIGHT
THE BRIDE WORE BLACK LEATHER

* *available from Severn House*

THE HOLY TERRORS

Simon R. Green

SEVERN
HOUSE

First world edition published in Great Britain and the USA in 2024
by Severn House, an imprint of Canongate Books Ltd,
14 High Street, Edinburgh EH1 1TE.

severnhouse.com

British Library Cataloguing-in-Publication Data
A CIP catalogue record for this title is available from the British Library.

ISBN-13: 978-1-4483-1163-7 (cased)
ISBN-13: 978-1-4483-1164-4 (e-book)

All Severn House titles are printed on acid-free paper.

Typeset by Palimpsest Book Production Ltd.,
Falkirk, Stirlingshire, Scotland.
Printed and bound in Great Britain by
TJ Books, Padstow, Cornwall.

Praise for Simon R. Green

"The story here . . . is so strong"
Booklist on *Not of This World*

"A blast for urban-fantasy readers looking for a broken
fourth wall riddled with dry-witted commentary,
evil getting its just deserts, and the good walking
away to fight the good fight"
Library Journal on *Not of This World*

"Features . . . one of the snarkiest antiheroes to
ever front an urban fantasy series, turning the
murder and mayhem up to 11"
Library Journal on *What Song The Sirens Sang*

"A wonderfully imagined setting . . . Perfect fare for
fans of urban fantasy, thrillers, or caper novels"
Booklist on *A Matter of Death and Life*

"A treat . . . Exciting, witty, and stuffed full of fun"
Booklist on *The Best Thing You Can Steal*

"Clever worldbuilding"
Publishers Weekly on *The Best Thing You Can Steal*

"Intriguing . . . Green offers enough to please series
fans and hook newcomers, while posing new mysteries.
X-Files devotees will be satisfied"
Publishers Weekly on *Buried Memories*

About the author

Simon R. Green was born in Bradford-on-Avon, Wiltshire, where he still lives. He is the New York Times bestselling author of more than seventy science fiction and fantasy novels, including the Nightside, Secret Histories and Ghost Finders series, the Ishmael Jones mysteries, the Gideon Sable series and his brand-new Holy Terrors mystery series.

The Stonehaven town hall wasn't much to look at. Just a sturdy old building with upright walls, tall narrow windows, and a steeply slanting slate roof. It had survived years of wear and weather, and any number of town planning fads and fancies. A simple hall for a small country town, always ready to serve a useful purpose.

But when the sun went down and the night came creeping in, the hall took on a grim and brooding look, as though some deep, dark aspect was stirring in its sleep. And townspeople who were happy enough to use the building for all manner of cheerful activities during the day showed a distinct tendency to hurry on by with eyes averted, as though not wanting to draw attention to themselves. Because everyone in the town had seen something, or heard some story, or felt the pressure of unseen watching eyes. The hall at night was something to be avoided. The kind of place it wasn't wise to turn your back on.

Stonehaven town hall was an old building, with perhaps a little more history than was good for it. And a sense of something bad waiting to happen.

ONE

The Most Haunted Hall in England™

And to that quiet little town in the middle of nowhere, on a bright sunny day in late autumn, came Alistair Kincaid, newly appointed bishop to All Souls Hollow, in London. He arrived in Stonehaven by train and walked unhurriedly through the town, enjoying its old-fashioned terraces and traditional cottages fashioned from the local creamy-grey stone. Most were adorned with attractively carved wooden shutters, or lattices covered in flowers and trailing vines. It was all very picture-postcard perfect, and would probably have felt quite pleasant and friendly, if there had been anyone around. But the streets were empty, and almost unnervingly quiet as the evening drew on; and when Alistair finally entered the hall car park, he wasn't that surprised to find it entirely deserted. Not a car to be seen in any of the neatly marked bays; and this in the kind of old country town where parking spaces were always going to be in great demand. He stopped just inside the entrance, and looked thoughtfully at the town hall. He couldn't shake off a quiet but definite feeling that something was looking back at him.

The occasional vehicle passed by behind him, but none of them so much as slowed down to investigate the car park. In fact, it sounded like the cars actually speeded up as they hurried off to be somewhere else. Alistair studied the open space as it stretched away before him, and decided it felt not so much empty as abandoned. Not a solitary figure walking through it, even though the car park was situated right in the middle of town. Alistair's eyes narrowed as he fixed his gaze on the town hall. He didn't normally think of himself as superstitious, but something about the entirely ordinary building was raising all the hackles on the back of his neck. Like a cold caress from an unknown hand.

And then a cheerful and very feminine voice rang out behind him, and he almost jumped out of his brogues.

'Hello there! You must be the famous God-botherer, from all those dreadful morning television shows!'

Alistair took his time turning around, just to make it clear he wasn't in any way startled or upset, and then nodded politely to the impossibly glamorous figure advancing toward him with a predatory grin and cheerful, sparkling eyes. He nodded politely.

'And you must be the celebrated Ms Hunt. Star of stage, screen, and supermarket checkout magazines. I'm glad to see you found your way here without any trouble.'

'Oh please, darling, call me Diana. Everybody does! If we're going to be guests on this godawful ghost-hunting show, we'd better start off as friends, because we're going to need all the support we can muster to get through this nonsense with a straight face.'

She thrust out a hand, with all the air of minor royalty bestowing a favour, and Alistair shook it solemnly. Diana had a strong, firm grip, that lingered just a little longer than Alistair was comfortable with. And then the two of them just stood there and looked each other over, trying to figure out how much use they could be to each other.

Alistair Kincaid was a handsome man in his late twenties, who always wore the same dark suit and dog collar as a kind of armour; to ward off anyone who thought they could take advantage of a bishop of such tender years. His smile was warm and his eyes were kind which, together with his classical features, had helped make him the popular face of modern Christianity on many a morning television programme. Selling his religion, to people who weren't sure they needed or even wanted it. His rimless granny glasses helped take the edge off his good looks, in a winning sort of way.

Diana Hunt was a tall, striking woman in her early thirties, almost bursting out of her sleek and fashionable dress. The emerald gown made a pleasing contrast to her long dark hair, and Alistair knew just enough to recognize her shoes cost more than he made in a year. Her familiar and very attractive face was backed up by a strong bone structure, under makeup so extravagant it had a character all of its own. But her broad smile seemed real enough and her dark eyes gleamed with a teasing mischief, just waiting to break out at a moment's notice.

'You're the new bishop of that hellhole borough in London, aren't you?' she said chattily. 'I wouldn't walk through that area on a bet, even if I was wearing a chainmail basque and carrying a loaded chainsaw in each hand.'

'All Souls Hollow is something of a poisoned chalice, as parishes go,' Alistair said easily. 'Not so much a rough area, more like a demilitarized zone. But Christ came to walk among sinners, and those who needed him.'

'Then it's no wonder you ended up on all those morning talk shows,' said Diana. 'Never any shortage of sinners sitting on those sofas. And that's just the hosts.'

'I see you got the same memo I did, not to bring any luggage,' said Alistair, pleasantly but determinedly changing the subject.

'I was assured I wouldn't need anything,' said Diana. 'Just as well, really, given that I had to walk all the way here from the station. If I'd known it was going to be such a hike, I wouldn't have chosen such fashionable heels.' She shook her head firmly, and her great mane of dark hair danced languorously for a moment. 'Never trust a television producer, darling. They all have their consciences surgically removed, right after they sign their first contract. I thought I'd be able to pick up a few necessities here in town; but it seems they lock all their doors and roll up the pavements the moment the sun hits the horizon.'

Alistair waited politely, to be sure she'd finished. 'I did find the streets just a little quiet.'

Diana grinned suddenly. 'Aren't you going to say *too quiet*?'

Alistair couldn't help but smile back. 'I might, if we were in a horror movie, rather than a television ghost-hunting show. And a one-off special Live! episode at that. It is good to meet you, Diana. I admired your performance in the *Miss Marple* mystery last week. That is the same outfit you wore in the show, isn't it?'

'You've got a good eye, Bish,' Diana said approvingly. 'First rule for appearing on television: grab everything that isn't actually nailed down on your way out, because you can be sure the production company will stiff you on the residuals.'

'I thought you made an excellent murderer,' said Alistair.

'I always go for the bad girls, darling. They get all the best lines.'

'I've seen you in a lot of things,' said Alistair. He wasn't sure he had, but it seemed a safe enough thing to say. 'I don't think I've ever met anyone famous before.'

Diana shrugged easily, which did some very alluring things to her figure. And Alistair had no doubt that she knew it.

'I'm just a jobbing actress, darling. Everything from the West End stage to daytime soaps; from *Macbeth* to *The Mousetrap*, from Bond to *Star Wars*. Wherever there's a need for talent and glamour, there you'll find me, hogging the spotlight and looking damned good doing it.'

Alistair nodded politely. 'I'm afraid my job doesn't allow me much leisure time. You're lucky I always make an exception for Agatha Christie.'

'And I've seen you on far too many of those empty-headed morning shows,' said Diana. 'Displaying Christian good cheer to people who probably only just lurched out of bed. I've never been too sure what you were doing there. I mean yes, I get it that you're very popular with housewives, and women of a certain age, and the more cloistered parts of the gay community. You always come across as very sincere, which helps to separate you from nearly everyone else on those shows. The relentlessly cheerful hosts, with their plastic surgery faces and stapled-on smiles, and guests who only appeared to publicize a new show, or some reinvented version of themselves. Guaranteed free from sex or drugs or whatever else it was that derailed their career in the first place.'

'I suppose I'm there to sell the advantages of faith,' Alistair said calmly. 'Except I'm not in it for the money.'

'Clearly, darling,' said Diana. 'Or you wouldn't let yourself appear in public wearing a suit from Undertakers Rejects. Let alone guest on a show like *Spooky Time!*'

'I go where I'm sent,' said Alistair. 'Where I'm needed. That's the job.'

Diana's eyes lingered over his broad chest and shoulders. 'You look very fit,' she said. 'For a bishop.'

'I used to row a lot at Oxford,' said Alistair. 'But I had to let that go when my religious studies took over. Even in those days, I was being fast-tracked in the church. I do still try to stay in shape.'

'Is there a Mrs Bishop?' Diana said artlessly. 'I thought all you C of E types had to have some decorative other half, to make the tea and hand round the cucumber sandwiches.'

'It's hard to find time for a personal life,' said Alistair, 'when there's always so much work waiting to be done. Are you married?'

'Oh, I've had several husbands, darling; some of them my own. I have a very romantic nature, and no inhibitions worth the mentioning, but I am currently in between matrimonial misadventures.'

'You did make quite a splash recently,' Alistair said carefully. 'When you allowed yourself to be photographed as part of a campaign for *Don't Wear Fur*. Just you, with no clothes on, hugging a large teddy bear to preserve your modesty. Was the nudity really necessary?'

'That photo got me on the front pages of all the dailies, darling,' said Diana. 'Including the *Financial Times*. If the campaign had wanted tact and good taste, they wouldn't have come to me. And besides – in my business, once you get to a certain age, it becomes vitally important to remind people that you're still impossibly good-looking. And to convince certain casting agents that you're still extremely bookable.'

Alistair smiled. 'I thought you looked amazing. And it was for a very good cause.'

'Causes come and go, but glamour is forever!' said Diana. 'Tell me, Bish: how did someone like you end up as part of the morning television circus?'

'No one else wanted the job,' said Alistair. 'The church decided it needed a friendly face on television and asked for volunteers, and everyone else had the good sense to take one step backwards. I didn't react quickly enough, so I got pushed into it. And, rather to my surprise, I turned out to have a gift for television. Though I have to admit, of late I don't seem to be attracting as much attention as I used to. The public can be very fickle.'

'You don't have to tell me that, darling,' said Diana. 'You throw your heart and soul into making the shallow little bastards love you, and the next thing you know they've thrown you over for the next pretty young thing.'

Alistair tactfully turned his attention back to the town hall. Diana moved in beside him, and pressed her shoulder companionably against his.

'Gloomy-looking dump, isn't it?' she said.

'I can't say it seems particularly welcoming,' said Alistair.

'Does it feel haunted, to you?' Diana said interestedly.

Alistair shrugged. 'I wouldn't know what a haunted building should feel like.'

'Really?' said Diana. 'I would have thought things like that were your bread and butter.'

'My interest is in the after-life,' Alistair said kindly. 'There's a difference.'

Diana scowled at the hall, and turned up her attractive nose.

'Reminds me of certain low-budget horror movies – roles my agent occasionally bullies me into accepting, when work is scarce and the creditors are baying at my heels. The kind of film where you just know someone wearing a monster mask is going to jump out of the shadows and threaten you with an electric hedge-trimmer.'

'There might not be any ghosts here,' Alistair said thoughtfully. 'We could be dealing with a *genius loci*.'

'I don't do the Latin, dear,' said Diana. 'Unless it's old school horror, and then I just fake it.'

'It means spirit of the place,' said Alistair. 'Some locations are just bad, without the need for human evil to contaminate them.'

'Well, you're packed full of cheerful notions, aren't you?' said Diana.

'Just trying them out for size, before the show begins,' said Alistair.

Diana glowered at the hall, as though warning it not to get ideas above its station.

'The whole thing looks like an ambush waiting to happen. Good thing I've got you here, to defend me.'

'You don't seem to me like the kind of woman who needs defending,' said Alistair.

They smiled at each other, until Diana's dazzling display made Alistair feel distinctly out-smiled. He stopped trying to compete, and changed the subject again.

'It was good of the production company to pay for our rail tickets.'

'Hah!' Diana said loudly. 'If we really mattered to them, they would have put their hands in their pockets and lashed out for chauffeur-driven limousines. Free rail tickets are what you offer when you can't get the kind of guests you want, and have to settle for whoever's available.'

'From the more affordable end of the spectrum, I'm guessing,' said Alistair.

'Got it in one, Bish.' Diana shot him a look, from under heavy eyelashes. 'What made your church decide you belonged in a downmarket reality show like *Spooky Time!*'

Alistair appreciated the amount of sheer venom she was able to put into her voice, every time she pronounced the show's title.

'Am I to take it you don't much care for the programme?'

'Of course not,' said Diana. 'I've seen it. If this show was any more staged, everyone would be wearing tights and spouting blank verse. The whole affair should come with a health notice: *Warning, may contain nuts.*'

'At least you've got some idea of what to expect,' said Alistair.

Diana shot him a sharp look. 'You've never watched a single episode of the show you've agreed to appear on?'

'I'm only here because of pressure from above,' said Alistair. 'My superiors thought guesting on a popular mainstream show like this might help my audience appeal. It's been a long while since my church could field anyone on television that the public would pay attention to.'

'And you think you can put out a positive message, by

appearing on a show like this?' said Diana. 'You do know what *Spooky Time!* is all about?'

'Some sort of documentary series, I was told,' said Alistair. 'Investigating potentially haunted locations.'

'They wish,' said Diana. 'Nothing so civilized, darling. Like most reality TV shows, actual reality doesn't get a look-in. It's all carefully constructed, in advance . . . Like a game show, only with the emphasis on screams rather than laughs, and no big prizes at the end.'

'So nothing in the programme is real?'

'Not if the producers can help it. *Spooky Time!* is basically light-hearted entertainment for the hard of thinking and particularly credulous, in which celebrities and personalities are escorted around supposedly haunted settings, and encouraged to react to nothing very much in suitably dramatic ways. You know, lots of jumping at shadows and pointing at things off camera. Shouting *Did you see that?* and *What was that noise?* There's never any real danger, or even a hint of a manifestation. It's more like the ghost-train ride at the seaside. Basically *Spooky Time!* is all about mood and atmosphere, and seeing how many times the show can make its audience jump for no reason at all. Just be grateful you won't have to eat kangaroo offal.'

Alistair wasn't entirely sure he understood that last segue, but let it pass.

'According to the publicity handout I was sent, the show has its own celebrity psychic?'

'Leslie Derleth,' said Diana, her mouth twisting unattractively. 'Calls himself a medium, but I can remember when he was just a glorified mind-reading act, with lots of carefully planted stooges in the audience.'

'You mean he fakes it?'

'Trust me, darling, he's no more real than anything else on this show. Everyone involved in *Spooky Time!* is some kind of performer.'

'Not me,' Alistair said firmly. 'Whatever reactions I may show to the camera, I assure you they will always be strictly genuine.'

'With an attitude like that, you'll be lucky to get any time in front of the cameras,' said Diana. 'They'll just cut to someone else who's being more dramatic. It's only a game, darling; you have to play along if you want to be a part of it.'

Alistair looked at her thoughtfully. 'Why do you think the producers chose us, to be their guests?'

Diana smiled broadly, happy for a chance to show off her insider gossip. 'Once upon a rating war, my dear Bish, *Spooky Time!* was one of the more successful ghost-hunting shows. Must-see television for the more gullible end of the market. But you can only promise so much without delivering, before the audience starts to feel it's been had. The show's viewing figures have dropped off a cliff in recent times, and the producers are desperate to claw their ratings back, which is why they came up with this whole "Live broadcast from inside a haunted hall!" idea.'

'Will you be faking your reactions?' said Alistair.

'If that's what it takes to keep all eyes fixed on me,' Diana said happily. 'I will point and shriek and grab people's arms with the best of them, until half the home audience are hiding behind their sofas or watching through their fingers. It's called acting, dear. And remember, once the cameras go live, it's every celebrity for themselves. Underplay your role and the rest of us will rush to trample you underfoot. There's no mercy to be found on reality TV; it's all about fame and fortune. Or, on this show, just the fame. I personally will be reacting so strongly, people at home will think they're viewing in 3D.'

And then both of them looked round sharply, as a loud and professionally trained voice hailed them from behind.

'Bishop Kincaid! And Diana Hunt! So good of you to arrive early!'

Alistair and Diana turned to face the newcomer, a young woman with very dark skin, a lively smile and sparkling eyes. She crashed to a halt before them, like a general come to inspect the troops. She was in her late twenties, but trying hard not to look it, and bubbling over with personality. She wore a black-and-white polka-dot catsuit, complete with white plastic knee-length boots, the whole Sixties look topped off by having her hair piled on top of her head in a towering beehive.

'June Colby,' Diana murmured in Alistair's ear. 'Host and producer of the show. Do try and act like you recognize her, because she'll be awfully upset if you don't.'

June's big smile never wavered once as she shook both their hands in a brisk and professional manner.

'Good to meet you, Ms Colby,' said Alistair. 'I'm sure this will be a very interesting experience for all of us.'

'Love the whole retro thing, darling,' said Diana.

'I know, it's a bit much,' said June. 'But this is what the audience likes, bless them, so I just grit my teeth and go along. And it does help me stand out.' She raised a hand to pat carefully at one side of her beehive, as though to reassure herself it wasn't tilting. 'You would not believe the maintenance that goes into making this stupid thing behave. Interior scaffolding, a whole bunch of long steel pins, and enough hairspray to frighten the life out of the ozone layer.'

'Doesn't that make it rather uncomfortable, Ms Colby?' said Alistair.

'Like you wouldn't believe. And please, call me June. We're all friends together on this show.'

Alistair caught a brief look on Diana's face, suggesting that wasn't what she'd heard, but it was quickly replaced by a professional smile.

'Of course, darling!' Diana said brightly. 'I just know we're all going to be the best of chums! So, what's the plan for tonight?'

'Oh, we like to keep things free and open,' June said easily. 'There is a format to follow, but feel free to contribute whatever you think helps. Just be yourselves, in a loud and dramatic way.'

'Format?' Alistair said carefully.

'Much like the usual, only more so,' June said briskly. 'We'll start with a stroll around the hall, pointing out things of interest and telling each other ghost stories, while ostentatiously flinching away from the more menacing-looking shadows. At some point my pet medium will go into his trance and have a heart-warming little chat with someone who isn't there, followed by some spine-tingling but suitably vague predictions. And as the night turns into morning, we will ratchet up the tension to something just short of controlled hysteria; and then the locks on the doors will open . . . And we all rush out into the light of day and go into the big hug, so everyone can get all tearful and supportive at having survived such a terrible experience. Simple as that. Stick to the format, and it will see you through.'

'It sounds . . . rather contrived,' said Alistair.

'That's what makes it work,' said June.

'I could put together a better show with a box of Lego bricks,' said Diana.

June's professional good cheer vanished in a moment, and she stared coldly at Diana.

'A lot of thought and hard work has gone into constructing a format that works, and that the audience wants to see followed. You just take your cues from me, and everything will work out fine.' She quickly put her game face back on, and hit Alistair with her most charming smile. 'Now then, we have to wait for two more guests to turn up, before we can get started. I expect things to get really thrilling, once we're locked inside that hall from dusk to dawn!'

'We're going to be incarcerated inside the hall all night?' said Alistair. 'There was nothing about that in your contact letter.'

'But there was a great deal about it in the contract you signed,' said June. 'It's not my fault if you can't be bothered to read the small print. The pre-programmed locks will slam shut the moment we're inside, and won't open again till morning. Just to add that special extra charge to the atmosphere!'

'So once we're in there, we can't get out?' said Alistair.

Diana smiled brilliantly. 'Smell the drama, darling.'

Alistair looked at June for a long moment, and then turned to face the hall.

'Diana and I have been studying our new home away from home, and I have to say it doesn't feel the least bit welcoming.'

'That's probably because it isn't,' said June. 'You are looking at the most haunted hall in England, and that is officially certified, by Guinness. Crammed with ghosts from wall to wall, and absolutely saturated with skin-crawling phenomena. Everything we need for a really good show!'

'Could you provide us with a few examples of what we'll be encountering?' said Alistair.

June laughed happily, and clapped her hands together. 'Of course: history and background! Forewarned is forearmed, so you'll know what to brace yourselves for.' She frowned prettily as she concentrated. 'Originally built by public subscription, back in 1910, these days the hall is just a building for hire. And tonight; it's all ours. *Spooky Time!* rules!'

'And the hall's owners don't mind us telling the whole world that their building is infested with ghosts?' said Diana. 'Won't that make it just a bit difficult for them to rent it out in the future?'

'The hall is currently owned by the town council,' said June. 'And they don't give a damn. They've been trying to sell the place for years, but no one will touch it because of its reputation. So now they're happy to take whatever money they can get.'

'But what is it that makes this particular building so scary?' said Alistair. 'What kind of hauntings are we talking about?'

June shot him a quick look that suggested guests should know their place, but quickly replaced it with her professional smile and soldiered on.

'According to local stories, the hall is home to all manner of supernatural goodies. It's got everything! All kinds of spooks and spectres, from Hooded Monks to Ladies in White. Reappearances of historical events, so real you can walk around inside them and even take home souvenirs. Weird figures walking through walls, awful faces peering out of windows, and strange lights and sounds late at night, long after everyone has gone home. There are cold spots to make you shudder, movements in the shadows, and voices that will murmur in your ear when you least expect them. You are looking at spook central!'

'Then why have we never heard of any of this before?' Diana said sweetly.

'Because it's all just local stories,' said June. 'They don't travel well.'

'Has anyone ever performed a serious investigation?' said Alistair. 'I mean, a proper scientific inquiry, designed to turn up solid evidence? Because I have to say . . . most of your stories sound pretty generic to me.'

June shrugged. 'Who knows, who cares? All that matters is, we have more than enough material to work with.'

Alistair nodded to Diana. 'At least now we know why the show's producers were able to hire the hall so easily.'

'You don't know the half of it, darling,' said Diana, smiling mischievously. 'I did some background research before I came down here. This hall is quite staggeringly available because two weeks ago a man working inside it dropped dead. And the look on his face suggested he died of stark terror . . .'

Alistair looked sharply at June. 'Is this true?'

'A man did die,' said June, just a bit defensively. 'But there's nothing for you to worry about.'

She broke off, as Alistair's frown became increasingly cold. 'You expect us to go ghost-hunting, in a building where a man has just died? At best, that is seriously disrespectful.'

'Oh please!' said June, giving him cold stare for cold stare. 'A sudden unexplained death is the gold standard for this kind of show! You mustn't take it to heart! Most of the settings we visit come with some kind of death attached, because that's what happens in every building that's been around for a while. I mean, get a few drinks inside any hotel manager, and they'll tell you they expect a dozen or so deaths every year. So whatever room you're staying in, you can be pretty sure someone has died in it.'

'I'm just happy if the bed isn't still warm,' said Diana.

'We have been generating major publicity, for this special live broadcast,' June said forcefully. 'Very definitely including the recent and possibly suspicious death; because it's all about getting our audience worked up into the proper state of mind.'

'Isn't that a little cold-blooded?' said Alistair.

June shrugged, and just like that her charming smile was back in place.

'We use what we're given. If it hadn't been the dead man, it would have been something else. It's all just grist for the publicity mill.'

'What about the man's family?' said Alistair. 'Won't they be upset over your exploiting their loved one's death?'

'They're not in any position to make a fuss,' said June.

Alistair drew himself up, and just like that there was something in his gaze that would have made anyone else look away.

'I am not taking part in any show that's prepared to trample over innocent people's feelings. Feel free to sue; my church has very big lawyers.'

'So do we,' said June, entirely unmoved. 'I personally made sure we tracked down all the family members, and had them sign agreements saying they're happy for us to go ahead. Funerals can be very expensive, these days . . . So, get off your high horse, Bishop; they signed away all their rights to object, so we can say anything we like.'

'I still don't approve,' said Alistair.

'And I still don't care,' said June. She appeared as buoyant as ever, but there was cold steel in her voice. 'Do what you've agreed to do, or we will sue; and you personally, Bishop, not your church. Because it's your signature on the contract.'

'I knew I should have checked the terms more carefully,' Alistair said to Diana.

Diana patted his arm, in a slightly more than comforting way.

'When this is all over, remind me to recommend you a good agent, darling.'

'Our pet medium will make contact with the dead man at some point,' said June. 'Get his side of the story, and maybe even a hint or two about what scared him so badly.'

'Is there anything you won't stoop to?' said Alistair. He was honestly curious.

'Of course not,' said June. 'I'm a television producer.'

Alistair turned back to Diana. 'Is there anything more about this hall that I ought to know about?'

Diana didn't even glance at June. 'According to reports in the local press, the dead man was one Albert Matheson, caretaker. Well into his late seventies, with a long history of heart problems. According to his family, his death didn't come as anything of a surprise.'

'But there was still that awful look on his face,' June said stubbornly. 'And the coroner said he couldn't be a hundred per cent sure what killed him. Come on, people; we have to work with what we're given. It comes with the territory.'

Alistair turned his attention back to the hall. 'Has anyone ever attempted a blessing, or a cleansing?'

'Oh, several times,' said June. 'For all the good it did them.' She brightened suddenly and clapped her hands together. 'But we have a bishop! One up to us! Would you be willing to perform an exorcism, live on camera? And I mean give it the full monty . . . Splash the holy water around, chant some Latin, and do the whole, "The power of Christ compels you!" thing. I loved that bit in the movie.'

Alistair looked at her. 'Real exorcisms aren't anything like that.'

'They would be if I was running things,' said June.

Alistair shook his head firmly. 'Exorcisms should never be attempted lightly. And anyway, I would need official permission from my church, which could take weeks to organize.'

June hit him with her most winning smile, clearly believing she could still overwhelm him with her celebrity glamour.

'But you must admit, it would make for truly impressive television. Good defeating Evil, live on air! Think of the publicity, for you and your church. People would be lining up to hire you.'

Alistair met June's smile with an unwavering gaze, so she just shrugged and moved on.

'Well, you're no fun. If you don't feel up to it, I'll just get our pet medium to fake something. Our audience wouldn't know the difference anyway. I once sprinkled some cottage cheese around and called it ectoplasm, and we got the best ratings ever.'

Alistair looked at Diana. 'I find all this open cynicism really quite dispiriting.'

'I mourn for our media generation,' said Diana. 'But you can't have show business without the show.' She shot a pointed glance at June. 'Though if you keep promising steak and can't even supply the sizzle, you shouldn't be surprised when your viewing figures plummet.' She turned back to Alistair. 'Always remember, darling; in this business nothing is ever what it seems. And you must admit, the established churches have a long history of putting on a good show. You can't preach to people until you've got their attention.'

Alistair nodded reluctantly. 'That is why I agreed to appear on television in the first place. To try and put a more human face on things.'

'Well,' said Diana, 'it is a very nice face.'

Alistair could feel himself blushing, and turned quickly away. But not before he caught the look of delight on Diana's face. He made himself concentrate on June.

'Do you believe in anything?'

'I believe in putting on a good show,' June said briskly. 'And giving our audience their money's worth.'

'As long as it doesn't cost us anything,' said a dispassionate voice behind them.

They all turned quickly, to find they'd just been joined by the show's resident medium. Middle-aged and unremarkable in his shabby suit and unpolished shoes, Leslie Derleth nodded briefly to everyone, but didn't offer to shake hands.

'Your reputation precedes you, Mister Derleth,' Alistair said politely.

'Leslie, please,' said the medium. 'We're all going to be good friends in front of the cameras, so we might as well start practising now. I told June we needed someone like you, to make this live broadcast work.'

Diana frowned. 'You and the bishop know each other?'

'More like we've followed each other round the same circuit,' said Leslie. 'There are only so many morning television shows. I am pleased to hear you taking this so seriously, Bishop.'

'That doesn't mean I am ready to endorse a medium,' Alistair said stiffly. 'My church has many strong things to say about false prophets.'

'What makes you believe I'm false?' said Leslie.

'Because you appear on shows like this,' said Diana.

Leslie actually smiled, briefly.

'And where have you been all this time?' June said sharply.

'I thought I'd hang back for a while, and listen to the conversation,' said Leslie. 'Get a feel for our celebrity guests.'

'And that right there is how they do it,' Diana said to Alistair. 'Eavesdropping for helpful details, to use against us later.'

'I just wanted to make sure you weren't the usual pushovers,' said Leslie. 'I always get the best material out of people who push back.'

Diana smiled brilliantly. 'Trust me, darling. I can push like you wouldn't believe.'

'Wait till you get inside the hall,' said June. 'You'd be surprised how quickly a spooky atmosphere can overwhelm you.'

Diana raised an elegant eyebrow. 'I do not "do" overwhelmed. I overwhelm. I've won awards for it.' She turned an entirely unimpressed look on Leslie. 'If you're such a hot medium, tell me something about my dead aunt.'

Leslie smiled calmly back at her. 'Of course. Which one?'

Diana stared at him blankly. Leslie nodded to June, and the two of them moved away so they could talk quietly together. Alistair moved in beside Diana.

'Don't let him get inside your head,' he said quietly. 'It wasn't an unreasonable guess, that you would have more than one deceased aunt.'

Diana nodded quickly as she pulled her charisma back about her. 'You watch yourself too, darling. You can bet he'll have studied every old YouTube clip of yours he can find, looking for things he can use to manipulate you.'

'My life is an open book,' said Alistair.

'Oh, so is mine, darling,' said Diana. 'Only I am a well-thumbed volume, with quite a few dog-eared pages.'

'Anyone I might know in the index?' Alistair said innocently.

Diana fanned herself with her hand. 'Why, Bish, I am shocked, I tell you, shocked!'

'I very much doubt that,' said Alistair.

Diana raised her voice to address June and Leslie. 'What are you two muttering about?'

Leslie gestured at the town hall. 'I was never happy about using this place. It has a bad history, and a bad feeling. Like a bear lurking in its cave, just waiting for its prey to venture within reach. This show has always been about poking bad situations with a stick to see what would happen. It was inevitable that eventually we'd run into something ready to poke back.'

'You really think this hall could be dangerous?' said Alistair.

Leslie didn't take his eyes off the building. 'Sometimes, the past isn't content to stay in the past.'

'He is so messing with your head, darling,' Diana murmured to Alistair.

'Very nice, Leslie, very dramatic,' June said briskly. 'But save the good stuff for the paying audience. The important thing is that this hall could be a gold mine, if we handle it properly. And you know we need this show to pay off, big-time.'

'Why?' Alistair said bluntly.

June stared at him steadily. 'Because if this live broadcast isn't a major success, it could be our last show. That's why we went for the best location we could find.'

'The best we could afford,' said Leslie.

Alistair frowned. 'I'm sure I was told *Spooky Time!* was a popular show . . .'

'One more time, darling,' Diana said patiently. 'Try and keep up. The whole ghost-hunting bit is on its way out. People stumbling around in the dark, and shrieking at things that only they can see, got old really fast, no matter how much they updated or reinvented themselves. *Spooky Time!* is the only one that still insists on clinging to its old format.'

'Because it works!' June said sharply. 'We can be successful again, with the right material. Our audience loves me! And Leslie.'

'Yes, dear, but that's celebrity love,' said Diana. 'Not the real thing. It never lasts.'

'A live broadcast from inside the most haunted hall in England – with all of us locked in overnight – will do the job!' June said stubbornly. 'And then we will be right back on top, where we deserve to be!'

'But if something should go wrong, we'd be trapped in there,' Leslie said quietly. 'With whatever it is that's recently killed a man. Once the time-locks close, no one can get through those doors to help us.'

'Nothing is going to go wrong!' June said loudly. She caught Alistair and Diana looking at her thoughtfully, and quickly wrapped herself in self-control again. 'Our technicians have been crawling all over this building for the last forty-eight hours, installing cameras, sound systems, and all the very latest in electronic toys.'

'What if none of your marvellous tech detects anything?' said Diana.

'That's where you come in!' June said sweetly. 'It will be your job to detect something, and be entertaining about it.'

'Do you have a script we can look at?' said Diana.

June pretended not to have heard that, and stared at the hall like a gunslinger weighing up a new opponent. Alistair moved in beside Leslie.

'Why is she dressed up like the Ghost of Sixties Past?' he said quietly.

'We tried her out in all kinds of different styles, back when we were starting,' said Leslie, just as quietly. 'Looking for something to grab the audience's eye. And unfortunately, this is the one they took to their hearts. It got an amazing response, possibly because it helped her stand out in the gloom, and the audience raised a hell of a fuss every time we tried something new, so we're stuck with it. I suppose it does have a certain visual impact.'

'Unlike your suit,' said Diana.

'It's June's job to be noticed,' said Leslie. 'Mine, to get things done. She holds the audience's attention, while I build and maintain the atmosphere. We make a good team.'

And then they all turned quickly, as a loud and cheerful voice hailed them from behind.

'I am getting really tired of being sneaked up on,' Diana growled.

Alistair had no trouble recognizing the new arrival as a professional comic. He had that relentless smile and full-on good cheer that came from facing live audiences on a regular basis, knowing they would eat him alive if he flinched. Well into middle age, he was a little less than average height, and a lot more than average weight, with a face that was more jowls than anything else. He was doing his best to hide his advancing years behind distressed jeans and a *Spooky Times!* T-shirt. He blasted his smile around the group,

and insisted on shaking everyone's hand in a distressingly
hearty manner.

'Hi there! Toby Marsh, supplying sparkling one-liners and
satirical barbs at trade prices. You bring the frights, and I'll
bring the laughs!'

'You're late,' said June.

'No, that's the people we'll be looking for,' Toby said
quickly. 'I'm always at my best live.'

'There is such a thing as trying too hard, darling,'
said Diana.

'You should know,' said Toby.

And then they all had to stand there politely as he ran
through his credits. Mostly stand-up appearances in halls and
theatres they'd never even heard of. Toby gave up when he
realized they honestly didn't care.

'That's the stand-up life,' he said bitterly. 'You spend years
on the road, hitting a new town and a new venue every night,
building your act and your reputation one joke at a time . . .
and then it all just slips away when you're not looking. Such
is fame. And age. I am hitting middle age, and middle age is
hitting back.'

Leslie looked at June. 'Was he really the best you could
find?'

'No one else was available,' said June. 'For the kind of
money we were offering. At least we can be sure he'll give
us his best new material; he needs this to be a success just as
much as we do.'

'Is there anyone more desperate than a professional funny
man looking for one last comeback?' said Diana.

'You're a fine one to talk,' said Toby. 'Have you still got
that teddy bear? Because it photographed better than you did.'

And then they all looked round again as heavy footsteps
approached from behind them. They turned pretty much as
one, and found themselves facing a small, wiry Indian woman
in her early twenties. Dressed in a multi-coloured sari, she
wore her hair scraped back in a strict bun; her pleasant face
was decorated only by a discreet nostril ring. Her tread was
so heavy because she was weighed down by two bulging
plastic carrier bags. She dropped them to the ground and

straightened her back with a low groan, before smiling around the group in a hopeful sort of way.

'Hello, I'm Indira Singh. Am I in the right place for the ghost show?'

'Our final guest!' June said loudly. 'Good of you to finally make an appearance, Indira.'

While the young Indian woman launched into a series of apologies, Diana eased in beside Alistair, responding to the blank look on his face.

'Honestly, darling, don't you know anyone? Indira is one of the new celebrity chefs. She came first on one of those big cooking contests on television, and ever since she's been trying to spin her ten minutes of fame into something like a career.'

'Would I be right in thinking this new career hasn't worked out too well?' Alistair said quietly. 'And that's why a celebrity chef is ready to appear on a ghost-hunting show?'

'See, you're getting the hang of it,' said Diana. 'Welcome to *Last Chances R Us*.'

June cleared her throat loudly to get everyone's attention, and then performed the necessary introductions to Indira. Who smiled and bowed politely to everyone.

'Sorry I'm late,' she said quickly. 'I got slowed down by the carrier bags. I didn't expect it to be such a distance from the railway station to the car park.'

'We did tell you not to bring anything,' said June. 'We can supply everything you need for an overnight stay.'

'Oh, but these are my special ingredients,' said Indira, grabbing up the plastic bags and hugging them protectively to her. 'So I can whip up some of my signature dishes for you, live during the show.'

'All based on recipes from your new book?' said Diana.

Indira beamed at her. 'Of course! Nothing like chasing round a town hall, searching for the not sufficiently departed, to raise an appetite!'

'Let me make it very clear to everyone,' June said sternly, 'That while I don't object to you plugging your work during the show, I expect you to be subtle about it. Or I will talk right over you.'

'And edit you out, if need be,' said Leslie. 'Guests have been known to disappear entirely from our shows, and it had nothing to do with supernatural forces.'

Indira looked a little crushed, and Alistair moved quickly forward to give her a supportive smile.

'Have you appeared on one of these ghost-hunting shows before?'

'Oh no,' Indira said quickly. 'This is my first time as a guest celebrity. I'm really all about the cooking.'

'It's all a matter of taste,' said Toby.

Indira looked at him blankly, and Toby pretended a sudden interest in the hall.

Leslie nodded to June. 'It's getting late. Give them the speech. You do it so well.'

'I should do,' said June. 'I've had enough practice.' She looked steadily around her assembled guests. 'All right, people, listen up! Always remember that *Spooky Time!* is first and foremost an entertainment show. You are therefore required to be suitably nervous and even scared, as necessary, while producing entertaining comments to make sure the audience remain engrossed in what's happening. We have a format, but no actual script; because we tried that and the audience could always tell. So keep it reasonably spontaneous. If anything should occur inside the hall that we can use, feel free to jump all over it; but don't get in each other's way. You'll all get your chance to be noticed.'

'What if nothing happens?' said Diana.

'Make something happen,' said June.

'Do you believe in ghosts?' Alistair said bluntly.

'I don't have the time,' said June. 'I have a show to run.'

'I take my medium skills seriously,' said Leslie. 'I had a very successful career, selling out packed theatres all across the country.'

'Only in places that hadn't seen you before,' said Diana.

'I don't believe in ghosts,' Indira said quietly, 'But I'm still scared of them.'

'Ghosts aren't scary,' said Toby. 'Live audiences are scary.'

'It's time we got this show on the road, people,' said June. 'Time and time-locks wait for no show.'

She stepped out briskly toward the town hall, and everyone else fell in behind her. She marched right up to the main doors, and one by one they all followed her into what appeared to be a perfectly ordinary town hall. And then the doors closed firmly behind them, and the time-locks slammed shut like the gates of Hell.

TWO
Did You Hear That?

Alistair turned a disapproving stare on the closed doors, and then looked around at his fellow guests, who seemed equally caught off guard. But when Alistair looked at June and Leslie, the two hosts were smiling quite happily. Alistair was just getting ready to raise his voice in a firm but dignified protest, when Toby grabbed hold of the door handles with both hands and gave them a good hard rattle. The doors didn't budge at all. Toby gave them a kick, just to make it clear how displeased he was, and then turned to scowl heavily at June and Leslie.

'What the hell is going on here?' he said loudly. 'Those doors slammed shut like the crack of doom!'

'I did warn you all,' June said cheerfully. 'Once the time-locks close, we are stuck inside this hall for the duration of the show. Which is basically from now until dawn tomorrow.'

'That's six forty-seven a.m.,' said Leslie. 'In case you were wondering.'

'We're trapped in here?' said Toby. 'You have got to be kidding!'

June stared him down with practised authority. 'Please don't fall apart this early; we've a long way to go till morning, and the show has only just started.'

Diana looked at her sharply. 'We're already on the air? We don't even get a chance to warm up?'

June gave her a pitying look. 'I would have thought a professional actress of your long standing would have had enough sense to read her contract properly.'

'Of course I didn't read it!' said Diana. 'That's what agents are for. And you can bet good money that I will be booting my soon to be ex-agent to the kerb the moment this show is over.'

Alistair moved quickly to position himself between Diana and June, before events could escalate. It felt like standing between two onrushing trains, but he held his ground and stared firmly at each of them in turn until they lowered their ruffled feathers.

'So this is it?' he said to June. 'The show is already under way?'

'Of course!' said June, showing the group her most cheerful smile. 'Isn't this thrilling? Thrown in the deep end, without a life-preserver, surrounded by spooky sharks and unseen phenomena; all of them no doubt more than ready to take a bite out of any one of us. This is live television; in your face and in the raw!'

'The on-site cameras started broadcasting the moment the time-locks closed,' said Leslie. 'Smile for the nice people watching, and try not to swear more than you have to.'

He sounded like everyone's favourite uncle; the man who would always understand what was happening, and be ready to explain it to the guests and the audience. Alistair studied the man dubiously, not sure whether this was the real person, or just a face Leslie put on for the cameras.

When Indira spoke, her voice was little more than a murmur.

'I don't know which scares me more. Being locked in, or surrounded by things we can't see.'

'The reason you can't see them is because there's nothing to see,' Toby said firmly. 'Don't let any of this get to you. I've faced opening nights packed with hecklers, drunks, and drunk hecklers; and I can tell you for a fact that people are the only really frightening things. Certainly a lot more than ghosties and ghoulies, which I don't believe in anyway.'

'The question is, do they believe in you?' said June. 'Now, will you all please pull yourselves together, and try to act like professionals. People are watching, and we need to get them on our side as quickly as possible. You can have your nervous breakdowns later, when you watch a repeat of the show and realize what a mess you made of what could have been your big break. I've nothing against a little honest emotion, in its place, but right now I need all of you to at least appear

charismatic and likeable.' She paused, and looked at Toby.
'Do the best you can.'

'I can scare an audience with the best of them!' said Toby.

'I know, darling,' said Diana. 'I've seen your act.'

'I paid for four celebrities!' said June. 'And I expect to get
my money's worth.'

'Are we celebrities?' Indira said diffidently. 'Or are we
personalities? I've never been entirely sure how you tell them
apart.'

'It's not rocket surgery, darling,' said Diana. 'A celebrity
can actually do something, while a personality is merely
famous for being famous. Which is why they don't last.' She
smiled smugly round the group. 'I'm sure you can all make
up your own minds as to which of us is which.'

'Saucer of cream for little miss cat . . .' said Toby.

'Blow me,' said Diana.

'Let's not go into full-on bickering right at the top of the
show,' Leslie murmured. 'Try to keep something in reserve,
so you've got room to build.'

'Of course, darling,' said Diana. 'We are professionals, after
all.'

Toby took a deep breath and looked around the hall. 'This
is not what I expected. I don't have any material to suit
this kind of setup. Where are your camera operators and sound
men?'

'Have you really never watched the show?' said June. 'We
dispensed with all that nonsense years ago. Their presence
distracted from establishing the proper spooky atmosphere.
We need our audience to feel that all of this is just happening,
while we happen to be here. We don't want anyone thinking
about camera tricks and sneaky edits.'

'Even though that's what makes for a good show,' said
Leslie.

'Never underestimate our audience,' June said firmly.
'They're smarter than you think.'

Leslie met her gaze calmly. 'You are talking about the same
audience that voted for an all-naked edition of the show?'

June sniffed. 'I should never have let you talk me out of
that. We would have killed in the ratings.'

'That's a dangerous road to start down,' said Leslie. 'You can never be sure where you'll end up.'

'I would have looked really good in just my beehive.'

'And all it would have cost us was our dignity.'

'Who needs dignity, when you've got ratings?'

'So,' Alistair said quickly, feeling like a referee trying to keep the peace in the middle of any number of fights. 'This is the most haunted hall in England? It all seems very ordinary so far.'

Diana sniffed. 'I still say we should have been given some warning. A girl should have a chance to touch up her makeup before she gets thrown to the lions.'

'Do you have room on there for any more?' said Toby.

Diana shot him down with a stare so cold it would have frightened a polar bear.

'One more word and I will drop-kick you through a wall.'

'No you won't!' June said quickly, flashing her professional smile around the group. 'We are all close friends and jolly good company, as long as we're in front of the cameras! It's important we present a united front to the ghosts, and the audience.'

Alistair cleared his throat loudly, and everyone turned to look at him. He put on his most reassuring smile, and kept his voice carefully calm and collected.

'Since the show is under way, and the audience is no doubt watching eagerly to see what we're going to do, why don't you explain exactly what it is you need from us, June?'

'Good thinking, Bish,' said Diana. 'First rule of any new acting project: know the ground rules.'

'First, you need to understand how the show works,' said June. She smiled meaningfully around the group. 'Above all, trust your host. Your host is wise and wonderful and knows many things.'

'Which she may or may not choose to share with you,' said Leslie. 'Just go along with June's way of doing things, and you'll avoid a lot of the bumps in the road. We have done this before. We know what works, and what doesn't.'

'Is there no room for individual input?' said Toby.

'Of course,' said June. 'As long as you do everything I tell you.'

She and Toby immediately fell to bickering again. Alistair tuned his hearing down, and took a thoughtful look around the hall. His first reaction was: *This isn't so bad.* There was nothing to suggest a supernatural threat, or any kind of other-worldly presence. He'd felt closer to the hereafter in his own church. He realized the argument had burned itself out, and turned his attention back to the other guests. They all seemed more than a little jumpy, in their own separate ways.

Toby was glaring about him, his whole body tense, as though bracing himself for the next unwanted surprise. Alistair was pretty sure that anything which even shouted Boo! at Toby was in for an unpleasant surprise. Indira was clutching her heavy shopping bags to her chest like some kind of armour, or at least something she could depend on. Her eyes were wide, and her mouth was pinched. Alistair felt a little worried about her. The show had barely begun, and already Indira looked like a child who'd wandered into adult territory. Diana was doing her best to look like she had everything under control, head held high and chest thrust out. Ready to meet any new threat with a smart remark and just possibly a kick in the penalty area.

Alistair sighed, inwardly. It was becoming increasingly clear to him that not only was he going to have to cope with what-ever the show could throw at him, but also protect and comfort his fellow guests. Though whether from unexpected phenomena or their own inner demons remained to be seen. Alistair always saw himself as the shepherd of his flock, whoever the flock happened to be, and he took his position seriously.

Because somebody had to.

He turned his attention back to the hall. It stretched away before him, an open, empty space entirely free of fittings and furnishings, fiercely illuminated by row upon row of fluores-cent tube lights. So much light, in fact, that there wasn't a shadow to be seen anywhere. The long featureless walls had been painted institutional grey, so that the place felt more like a prison than a town hall. There were no posters, artwork, or warning signs anywhere. Alistair was pretty sure that was because June had had them all torn down, in case they inter-fered with the impression she wanted the hall to make.

He glanced at the narrow windows, full of the last light of evening. He didn't need to check his watch to know it would be night soon, and then the hall would be surrounded by darkness. He didn't know why that thought bothered him, but it did. The bare wooden floorboards squeaked protestingly under his feet as he shifted his weight, and when he looked down he realized they hadn't been polished, let alone waxed, for some time.

Alistair looked back and forth, trying to work out why he was feeling increasingly disturbed. Possibly because there was nothing to suggest that this was a hall used by everyday people for ordinary reasons. It looked deserted and abandoned, because everyone else had more sense than to come here. Alistair's frown deepened, as he tried to get some kind of feel for the place, but it continued to evade him. As though there was nothing to get hold of. It was like looking at a man hiding his true feelings behind a mask.

'Anything wrong, Bish?' Diana said quietly beside him. 'That scowl really doesn't suit you.'

'The hall doesn't feel right,' said Alistair, just as quietly. 'But I'm damned if I could tell you why.'

Diana raised an elegant eyebrow. 'Language, Bish. I'm supposed to be the heathen around here.'

'And I expected to be the voice of reason on this show,' said Alistair. 'But something about this whole setup is playing merry hell with my nerves. I'm not seeing anything out of the ordinary, but I can't help feeling that we're not entirely alone here . . .'

Diana chuckled earthily. 'That's the cameras, darling, and all those fascinated eyes watching from their sofas, just waiting for something nasty to happen to us.'

'Oh, I'm used to that,' said Alistair. 'I've done my time on morning television.'

They shared a smile, for a moment.

'This light is a bit harsh, isn't it?' Toby said loudly. He was still doing his best to peer suspiciously in every direction at once. 'It's like being trapped inside a deserted call centre. Can't someone dial the glare down a bit?'

June glanced quickly at the overhead lights. 'They don't

exactly contribute to the atmosphere, do they? Our technicians should start shutting some of them down any moment now. Give us some nice spooky shadows to react to. You can never have too many shadows.'

Alistair nodded solemnly. 'Unless you're Cliff Richard.'

Diana raised an elegant eyebrow. 'That dates you, darling.'

'My mother was a big fan,' said Alistair.

'That explains a lot,' said Toby.

'You could try to appear a bit more impressed by your surroundings,' said June.

'I am trying to get into the spirit of things,' said Toby. 'But the hall isn't exactly cooperating. I'm surprised you didn't have your people decorate the place with cobwebs.'

'Oh, I can't be doing with those,' said June. 'We don't want to look like we're in some old-time movie. Start playing to your audience's expectations, and before you know it they'll be demanding scuttling rats and swooping bats.'

'I have never understood what is supposed to be so spooky about vermin,' said Leslie, with a barely suppressed shudder.

'They make you scream and want to climb on a chair,' said June.

He glared at her. 'It was just the one time!'

'This hall is quite astoundingly empty,' Alistair said quickly. 'Can I just point out that I'm not seeing even a few chairs for us to sit on?'

'I can't be on my feet all through the night!' Indira protested. 'Not after carrying these heavy bags all the way from the station.'

'Damn right!' said Diana. 'Since when do halls for hire come without even the most basic amenities?'

'Since the town council decided it wasn't going to spend a penny on this place that it didn't have to,' said Leslie. 'Whoever hires the hall is expected to bring whatever they need with them. But don't worry: we can supply all the usual comforts.'

Toby sniffed loudly, to make it clear to everyone how utterly unimpressed he was with absolutely everything.

'What do the locals use this dump for? Old-time dancing, and red-hot bingo sessions?'

'This hall provides a centre for all the usual local groups

and interests,' said June. 'During the day.' She pointed to the
far end of the hall. 'They've even got a raised stage for amateur
theatricals. Stairs round the back lead up to a dressing room
in the rafters.'

'Go on, Diana,' said Toby. 'Get up on the stage and show
us your versatility.'

'You couldn't afford me,' Diana said icily, before turning
her glower on June. 'I am not accustomed to appearing on
shows that can't even supply chairs for the talent to sit on! I
have my reputation to consider.'

'Of course there are chairs!' said June. 'And all the comforts
of home.'

'If this is your idea of comfort, I'd hate to see where you
live,' said Toby.

Indira surprised them all then with a snort of laughter.

June gestured at a side door, off to the right. 'Everything
you could possibly need to get through one night away from
home is tucked away there. We have kitchens, storerooms and
toilets.'

'Try not to get them mixed up,' said Toby. He looked quickly
round the group, and shuddered dramatically. 'Wow, tough
crowd . . .'

'You should know,' said Diana.

Alistair was about to perform another of his diplomatic
interventions, when suddenly and without any fuss the lights
started to go out. Everyone looked up and made startled noises,
as one by one the fluorescent tubes flickered and went out. In
just a few moments, half of the tubes had dimmed away to
nothing, and the light in the hall began to disappear. Everyone
moved closer together, as dark shadows pressed forward from
every side. Diana grabbed Alistair's arm and squeezed it hard.
He put a comforting hand on top of hers. He tried to think of
a suitable prayer, but nothing in his repertoire seemed to fit.
A growing gloom surrounded the group as the lights continued
to fade out.

Alistair looked quickly around him. Toby had placed himself
between Indira and the nearest shadows. Indira had dropped
her shopping bags, so she could close her tiny hands into fists.
June and Leslie were standing back to back, looking as though

they'd been sucker-punched. Alistair turned to Diana, and found she looked more angry than scared. She managed a quick smile for him, and removed her grip from his arm.

'Don't let this get to you, darling,' she said steadily. 'Taking out the lights is a standard opening tactic on shows like this. It's designed to catch everyone off balance, and see who will make the most dramatic noises. They're just messing with our minds.'

'You think this is down to June and Leslie?' said Alistair. 'They look as startled as the rest of us.'

'They're actors, darling. Just like me. Always putting on a performance for the cameras.'

June's head snapped round. 'This wasn't supposed to happen! The technicians were only supposed to reduce the glare, not let us disappear into the dark.'

'They're your people!' said Toby. 'Get them under control!'

June whipped out her phone, started to punch in a number, and then stopped and stared blankly at the screen. Leslie moved quickly in beside her.

'What is it? What's wrong?'

'There's no signal,' June said numbly. 'But reception was fine yesterday . . .'

'Who are you trying to call?' said Alistair.

'Our support staff,' said June. She shook her phone hard, but it didn't seem to help. 'Derek the director, and all his people. We set them up in a trailer in the car park. They have control over all technical aspects of the show, so Leslie and I can concentrate on managing the performances. Does anyone else have a signal?'

Alistair got out his phone, but it was dead in his hand. A quick glance around showed everyone else staring at their useless phones as though an old friend had betrayed them.

'I haven't got a single bar!' said Toby.

'How is that possible, in this day and age?' said Indira. 'Are we in a blind spot?'

'Of course not!' June snapped. Her professionally cheerful manner seemed to have deserted her. 'Or we'd never have chosen this location!'

Diana frowned at her suspiciously. 'Are you seriously saying this isn't one of your little tricks? Drop the lights to freak us out, and then jam all our phones so we're cut off from the world, just in case we were thinking of phoning a friend?'

'None of this is down to us,' said Leslie. 'It would be far too obvious; the audience would never buy it. We've always prided ourselves on running a subtle show.'

'And anyway,' said June. 'The one time we tried taking people's phones away, they all freaked out big time and we had to give them back.'

The whole group was standing close together now, staring out at the darkness. Barely a dozen of the fluorescent lights were still working, down the length of the hall. Alistair checked his pockets.

'What are you looking for?' said Diana.

'Matches,' said Alistair. 'Never know when you might have to light a candle, in my line of work . . .'

'Do you have a candle?' said Diana.

'Not on me, no,' said Alistair. 'But there must be something here I could burn.'

'Don't look at me,' said Diana. 'I always go commando.'

'I don't think I like this,' Toby said slowly. 'It feels like there's something watching us from the shadows . . .'

'Really not helping!' said Diana.

'I don't believe in ghosts,' Indira said loudly. 'I don't!'

'Look at the lights!' said Alistair.

They all stared at the ceiling. The tube lights had stopped going out. Everyone concentrated on the ones that were still lit, willing them to stay on, and finally relaxed a little and sighed heavily when nothing further happened. The shadows surrounding the group were disturbingly deep and dark, but at least they'd stopped creeping forward. Alistair gestured at the narrow windows.

'We've still got some evening light coming in. Though I don't know how long that will last. Is there a full moon tonight?'

'Would that mean anything?' said Indira.

'Let's hope not,' said Toby. 'Because if anyone starts getting seriously big and hairy, I didn't bring a razor.'

'Did anyone think to bring a torch?' said Alistair.

'We were told we didn't need to bring anything,' said Diana.

'There are candles in the kitchen,' said June. 'Now will you please all stop panicking, and going straight to the worst-case scenario! It's a bit early in the show for that.'

'We've lost a few lights, that's all,' said Leslie.

'And our phones aren't working,' said Indira.

'You mean we'll have to spend the evening talking to each other?' said Toby. 'The horror, the horror . . .'

Diana sniffed loudly and glowered at June. 'What kind of a show are you running, where you can't even keep the lights on?'

June didn't so much as glance at her. She and Leslie were busy studying the shadows that now filled most of the hall. Both hosts looked not only surprised, but genuinely disturbed, and Alistair had to wonder if they were really as in control of things as they liked to make out. He was also surprised at how quickly he'd given way to fear and alarm when the lights started going out. He was supposed to be the source of spiritual strength for this group. He made himself breathe steadily, and took comfort in an old saying from his seminary: *It doesn't matter how hard the world knocks you down, as long as you get up again.* He cleared his throat, and immediately everyone turned to look at him. Because there are no atheists in haunted houses.

'We have enough light to see by,' he said calmly, 'and I'm not seeing anything out of the ordinary for us to worry about. We've had a bit of a fright, but we're all perfectly safe.'

Diana looked thoughtfully at the ceiling. 'Does it strike anyone else as interesting, and not a little suspicious, that the remaining lights just happen to be spaced wide enough to cover all of the hall? Almost as though someone had arranged it that way . . .'

'Embrace your paranoia,' Leslie said calmly. 'It can come in very handy on a show like this.'

'The technicians must be on top of the problem,' said June. 'Or we'd all be standing around in the dark, using the bishop's matches to set light to each other. It is always possible that the director jumped the gun a little and got carried away.'

'In which case, you will no doubt find a few suitable words with which to reprimand him later,' said Leslie.

June smiled, and then lowered her voice. 'Never get mad at your director while you're still on the air.'

Toby scowled around him. 'I really don't care for all these shadows. It's like the hall is trying to scare us.'

'It's not that bad,' said Alistair. 'We have more than enough light to make sure nothing is creeping up on us.'

Diana shook her head. 'You had to go there, didn't you?'

'It does feel like there's something in the shadows,' said Indira. 'I don't like any of this.'

She sounded honestly upset, and Toby moved in beside her. He dropped the funny-man persona, so he could sound reassuring and comforting.

'Take it easy, Indira. There's nothing to worry about. If one more light so much as flickers, I will kick those doors open and lead the charge out of here.'

Indira shot him a grateful glance, and nodded quickly. She picked up her shopping bags again and hugged them like a child with a favourite toy.

Alistair kept his gaze fixed on June. She'd walked right up to the edge of the light and was staring into the shadows. He moved in beside her, just in time to hear her mutter to herself.

'Something's not right here . . .'

'I would have thought you'd be used to spooky settings,' said Alistair.

She nodded quickly and tried for her usual cheery smile, but couldn't quite bring it off.

'This wasn't in the script.'

'You mean format,' Alistair said solemnly.

Her smile seemed a little realer this time. 'Potato, tomato. Of course we planned to take the lights down at some point, to help build the atmosphere. But not this much, or so soon. We need enough light that the audience can see what's happening. I'm worried there might be a real problem with Derek and his people, and their equipment. That's the last thing we need.'

Diana moved in on June's other side, determined not to be left out of anything.

'I thought you always made a big deal about having infra-red cameras?'

'They only work in small doses,' said June. 'Run them too long, and the audience will turn off in droves.'

'Where are the cameras?' said Alistair. That felt like something he ought to know. 'Maybe you could use them to communicate with the director.'

June gestured vaguely around her. 'They're built into the walls. They have to be too small to see, or people start acting to them. This way, the guests can forget the cameras and just act natural.'

Leslie arrived to join them. 'I think if Derek or his people could have done something about the lights, they would have by now. There must be a major breakdown. Though whether it's to do with them, or the hall's antiquated electrical systems . . . Or possibly something unknown—'

'Don't go there,' June said sharply.

'Whatever it is,' said Leslie, 'no one can get in to help us. I did warn you, June, but you had to be all about the drama. How's that working out for you?'

'If I didn't know better, I'd say you were developing a spine,' said June. 'Not a good idea. I can always get another medium who knows his place.'

'Not for this show you can't,' said Leslie. 'Go talk to the nice director.'

June stalked forward to stand in front of the wall, and fixed an unseen camera with a glare that should have melted its internal workings.

'Derek! Get these lights back on, or your next job will be directing traffic in the middle of Wimbledon Common!'

'The problem is,' Leslie said confidentially to Alistair, 'we can talk to the director but he can't talk to us. We have to take it on trust that he's even listening.'

'In a real emergency,' Alistair said carefully, 'could the technicians override the time-locks and let us out?'

'Unfortunately, no,' said Leslie. 'Those are top-of-the-line security locks. We had to order them specially. We made a big deal out of that in the show's advance publicity, to add to the drama.'

'Whose bright idea was that?' said Diana.

Leslie didn't actually look at June. 'It seemed like a good idea, at the time.'

'I do comedy, not drama,' said Toby, as he and Indira joined them. 'And this is getting far too dramatic for my liking.'

'I just wanted a bit of an adventure, and a chance to push my new book,' Indira said accusingly. 'I thought this would be fun—'

'It will be,' Leslie said quickly. 'Once we get back on track. We just got off to a bit of a bad start, that's all.'

Diana looked at June, and raised her voice. 'Are you sure the director can see you?'

'Of course,' June said immediately. 'We use only the best technology on this show!'

'Then why are most of the lights still out?' said Toby.

June didn't look back at him. 'I'm working on it!'

'When you're dealing with a building this old, you have to allow for problems with the electric systems,' said Leslie. 'The council hasn't brought the wiring in this place up to speed for years.'

Alistair looked at him thoughtfully. 'I thought you said your technical people had been all over this hall?'

'They were supposed to have checked everything,' said June, as she came striding back to join the group. 'Something else I will have words about, once this show is over.'

'Maybe we could check the fuses?' said Toby. 'Or the circuit-breakers?'

'First, I have no idea where to look for them,' said Leslie. 'And second, even if we could track them down, would you have any idea how to fix what was wrong?'

Toby shrugged, in a way that suggested he thought he'd done everything that could reasonably be asked of him.

'Not as such, no. Maybe we should go and find some of those candles in the kitchen. Just in case.'

'I'm still worried about what's wrong with our phones,' said Indira. 'I've never been out of touch for this long. My messages must be piling up.'

'I doubt it's just us,' said Alistair. 'More likely, a mast has failed. We are way out in the sticks, after all. I'm sure they'll have things up and running again soon.'

'It must be wonderful to have such faith, darling,' said Diana.

'That's my job,' said Alistair.

Leslie moved in close beside June and lowered his voice. 'Whether we like it or not, the show is under way. Everyone is watching. We can't just stand around muttering to each other, or people will start to think we've lost control.'

'Some of them would probably like that,' said Diana. 'There's always a few that love it when things go wrong.'

'That is not happening on my show,' June said firmly.

'You'd better give our guests the other speech,' said Leslie.

'More rules and regulations?' said Toby. 'Oh joy.'

'Happy happy joy joy!' said Indira, just a bit unexpectedly.

June put on her cheery persona again, and smiled quickly round the group. It was a good performance, but Alistair could see the strain behind it.

'OK!' June said brightly. 'There are problems with the lights, but we can work around that. Now; it's important to remember that shows like this don't just happen. We have to make things happen. By seeing and hearing things off camera, and then reacting dramatically enough to sell them to the audience. So when someone starts something, I want to see the rest of you jumping in and being supportive. It's best if you all decide in advance just what your particular role is going to be. Toby, I need you to bring the funny. Diana, give us lots of emotion, and make it big.'

'There's another kind?' said Diana.

June ignored her, and fixed her gaze on Alistair.

'I want to see lots of religious action from you, Bishop. Prayers, blessings, and don't hold back when it comes to waving your crucifix around. You did bring a crucifix?'

'I think I might have one somewhere about my person,' Alistair said solemnly. 'Would you like me to invoke the Clear White Light, as spiritual protection?'

June looked at him, not sure whether she should be taking that seriously.

'Maybe later,' she said.

'Excuse me,' said Indira, hugging her shopping bags to her chest so she could raise one hand like a child at school. 'What do I do?'

'Be likeable, and vulnerable,' said Leslie. 'That's why we booked you.'

Indira lowered her hand. Going by the look on her face, she wasn't sure how to take that.

'We have to sell the atmosphere to the audience,' said June. 'Make them believe that something out of the ordinary is happening. If you seem convinced, the audience will be too.'

'So you're not expecting any real ghosts to turn up?' said Indira.

'They haven't bothered us for the last seven series,' June said sweetly.

Alistair cleared his throat again.

'You should take something for that,' said Diana. 'It's starting to sound painful.'

Alistair gestured for everyone to draw in a little closer. He nodded surreptitiously at the wall cameras, and spoke quietly to June.

'Given that everything we do is being broadcast live, do you really want to give away all your show's secrets?'

June smiled knowingly, and didn't bother to lower her voice. 'Derek will make sure the nice people at home only see and hear what we want them to. He can fade the mikes in and out, and use camera angles to force the audience's attention to where we want it. We also have a built-in delay, to give him plenty of time to make up his mind. We already agreed he should cover the show's opening with local voices from pre-recorded interviews, to help set the scene. He's also got a whole bunch of old documentaries on the hall's historical and supernatural history, which he can pick and choose from when we're not being interesting enough.'

'Shows like ours are made in the editing,' said Leslie.

'But we're supposed to be going out live!' said Diana.

June and Leslie exchanged a knowing smile, and Diana bristled at being made to feel like an outsider.

'We're only live when we choose to be,' said June, just a

little condescendingly. 'I doubt whether more than ten per cent of what we do will actually appear on the show. Unless you're all on really good form, of course.'

'There's nothing like a little incentive,' said Leslie.

'Derek can run vox pops with the locals, bits and bobs from old-time local news reports, and use them to either back up what we're doing, or hold the audience's attention when we're taking a break.' June smiled. 'We're selling the illusion of a live broadcast, that's all.'

'I feel oddly disappointed,' said Alistair. 'It's like going backstage at a magician's show and seeing how all the tricks are done.'

'I would have thought you'd feel relieved, to know for a fact that it's all bullshit,' said Toby.

'The hall feels scary,' said Indira. 'I don't like it. I haven't felt safe since I came in here.'

'Don't let it get to you,' said Toby. 'It's just television. We're all here with you! And it's a well-known fact that ghosts never go near groups of people, because they're scared of them.'

Indira gave him a look that said she knew he was just trying to cheer her up, but appreciated the effort.

Diana fixed Toby with a thoughtful look. 'So you don't believe in ghosts?'

'Hell no,' said Toby. 'I've died often enough on stage that I think I would have seen some by now. But, I am still perfectly ready to profit from them.'

'That is why we booked you,' said Leslie.

'I knew it wasn't for the laughs,' said Diana.

Alistair looked at Leslie. 'Do you believe in ghosts?'

'My gifts are real,' Leslie said carefully. 'Or at least, they used to be. Ever since I was a child, I could sense things no one else could. More than enough to convince me that we are not alone in this world. That there are worlds beyond our own.'

'Then why did you always plant so many stooges in your audience?' said Diana.

'Because the gift comes and goes,' Leslie said quietly. 'And I had a living to make.'

'You never made any serious money out of being a medium

until you joined up with me,' said June. 'I made you a success, and don't you forget it.'

'Like you'd ever let me,' said Leslie. 'You think I don't know you always refer to me as your pet medium?'

'Just as long as you come when I call,' said June. She smiled easily at her guests. 'Don't let him get ideas above his station. Whatever he does, he does to order on this show. If I tell him to make contact with a Headless Monk, or the man who died here recently, I know I can rely on him to produce a few minutes of suitable conversation with the not-entirely departed.'

June might be convinced her pet medium was a fake, but Alistair wasn't so sure. There was something in the man's voice, and in his eyes. Alistair didn't necessarily believe in mediums, but he was pretty sure Leslie did. He caught the man's eye.

'How is your gift, right now? Are you picking up anything that the rest of us should know about?'

Leslie met his gaze steadily. 'I wanted to use my gift to help people. But the more I abused it, on the stage and on this show, the less it would answer to me. On some of the shows June and I did, there could have been a whole crowd of ghosts dancing up a storm all around us and handing out spot prizes, and I still wouldn't have known a thing about it.'

'But what about here, and now?' said Alistair.

'It's just a show!' June said loudly. 'There's nothing here but us!'

Leslie looked slowly around the hall, his gaze calm and steady, as though the dark shadows were no barrier at all.

'I can feel death on the air,' he said quietly. 'Close, and getting closer.'

'Leslie!' June's voice cracked like a whip. 'That's enough!'

Leslie looked at her as though he'd forgotten she was there, and then shrugged and turned away, his hands thrust deep into his pockets.

'There are no ghosts here,' June said firmly to her guests. 'Just as well, really. They'd only get in the way.'

'Perhaps you need to have a little more faith,' said Alistair.

June smiled coldly. 'It would only get in the way.' She

smiled briskly round the group, and clapped her hands together like a teacher trying to organize a bunch of raucous children. 'All right, everyone! I want you to split up and go explore the hall. See what there is to see, and decide what it is you're going to bring to the show.'

The guests looked at each other and made no move to go anywhere. It was obvious none of them were happy at the thought of going anywhere on their own.

'Don't be such wimps!' June said encouragingly. 'Nothing is going to happen to you!'

'You didn't seem so sure about that when the lights were going out,' said Diana.

'That was then, this is now. All you have to do is spread out, and get a feel for where everything is. And above all, take the time to work out things to do later.'

'And what will you be doing?' said Diana. 'While we're off inventing bits of business, and fun moments, and generally doing your job for you?'

'I will be figuring out how to get this show back on track,' said June. 'We've only been here ten minutes and already the lights are playing up, the director is not listening to me, and my pet medium is off in a world of his own. Now listen up, people; I want everyone back here in half an hour, ready to hit the audience with something really startling, so we can get this show up and running!'

Indira nodded quickly at the side door. 'I'm going to check out the kitchens, drop off these increasingly heavy bags that seemed like such a good idea at the time, and see what kind of ovens they have here so I can prepare one of my famous meals.'

'You couldn't make us a cup of tea while you're there, could you?' said Toby.

Indira glared at him. 'Feminism. What a waste of time that was.'

She strode over to the side door. Toby shuddered dramatically.

'I was better off making jokes about killer ghosts.'

He headed for the side door as well. Without looking back, Indira raised her voice.

'Stay the hell out of my kitchen, or I will turn specific parts of your anatomy into spicy meatballs.'

'I'm just going to check out the facilities,' said Toby. 'First rule of show business: always know where the toilets are.'

Indira shouldered the side door open, and Toby hurried through after her. Diana smiled at Alistair.

'They're getting on nicely.'

'I could tell,' Alistair said solemnly. 'But I still think I'll avoid the spicy meatballs.'

June and Leslie moved off to one side and put their heads together. They seemed to have a lot to say to each other, with much shaking of heads and waving of hands, so Alistair just happened to drift casually in the same direction, until he was close enough to hear what they were saying while ostentatiously looking somewhere else.

'I will have Derek's balls on a skewer for this!' June said fiercely. 'How can anyone screw up turning off a few lights?'

'He might genuinely be having electrical problems,' said Leslie. 'That would explain why the lights haven't come back on again. And it did give us a good spooky start to the show.'

'But I'm supposed to be in charge here,' said June. 'How does all of this make me look?'

'Do you really want to know?' said Leslie.

Alistair jumped just a little, as he realized Diana had moved silently in beside him, and was eavesdropping just as shamelessly as he was. She flashed him a reassuring smile.

'I wouldn't take anything they're saying too seriously, darling. It all sounds a bit rehearsed to me.'

'You think they want us to overhear them?' said Alistair.

'Wouldn't surprise me in the least,' said Diana. 'It's all part of pointing the guests in the desired direction. I think everything that's happened since we walked in here has been part of the show; and I don't believe the audience has missed one single moment of our little dramas.'

Alistair frowned. 'But what about June giving away all the behind-the-scenes secrets on how the show is put together?'

'You think the audience doesn't already know?' said Diana. 'The celeb mags and women's glossies are full of that stuff.

No, we're just audience fodder, darling. Get used to the idea, because that isn't going to change.'

Alistair shook his head slowly. 'Is there anyone here I can trust?'

'Oh me, darling, absolutely,' said Diana.

She slipped an arm through his and led him away from June and Leslie. Alistair let Diana do it. He felt surprisingly comfortable in her company.

'So,' he said. 'What do you plan to do, to make this show interesting?'

'Be myself, of course,' she said cheerfully. 'I know how to hold an audience's eye, no matter what everyone else is doing.' She looked at him thoughtfully. 'Do you believe in ghosts, Bish?'

'I've had a few experiences that I can't explain.'

'Like what?'

Alistair took a moment to choose his words carefully. 'At my old church in Bristol, there was an old pipe organ. Sometimes it would start playing late at night, even though the place was locked up and nobody was there. And one time, I was called out to an old manor house to exorcize two old-time skulls that supposedly started screaming any time someone tried to remove them from the house to give them a decent burial. I'm pretty sure I was only there to provide the family with free publicity, as they opened their house to a paying public. And yet . . . I did get this odd feeling, during the ritual blessing, that only stopped when the ceremony had been completed.'

'Did the skulls stop screaming?' said Diana.

'Presumably,' said Alistair. 'Certainly I was never called back to try again. What about you?'

'Oh, I know lots of stories, darling,' said Diana. 'Most of them not suitable for religious company, so let's stick to the spooky ones for now. There's the dim figure that lurks in the wings of the Bristol Old Vic, but only when it's a Shakespearean production. Presumably some long-dead actor, still waiting for his cue to go on. Then there's the Liverpool theatre where the stage door is supposed to be guarded by the ghost of some old stage manager, who will only open the door to actors he thinks are talented enough. And there's a Glasgow theatre where one dressing room is never used, because it's still filled with the presence of some old star who won't give it up . . .'

Alistair raised a hand, to stop what promised to be an endless stream of supernatural narratives.

'And these are all things you've actually witnessed yourself?'

'Well, no darling; but they're stories everyone in the business knows.'

'Exactly,' said Alistair. 'Stories. And, I think, just a little too dramatic to be taken seriously.'

And then they both looked round sharply, as slow, deliberate footsteps made their way across the hall, heading towards them from the empty stage. The sounds drew steadily closer, and Alistair's skin prickled as he looked quickly back and forth, confirming there was no one at all present who could be making them. Each footstep sounded out clear and distinct, and yet Alistair couldn't hear any echo from them, despite the great open space of the hall. As though the footsteps weren't solid enough to make any real impact on the world.

Diana moved in close beside him, her shoulder pressed hard against his. She tried to say something, but the words wouldn't come. Alistair shot a quick glance at June and Leslie. They were standing close together, their shocked gaze fixed on where the footsteps appeared to be coming from. And then the sounds stopped.

Everyone stood very still. The hall was so quiet Alistair could hear Diana's heavy breathing beside him. And then the footsteps started up again, only this time they seemed to be coming from the other end of the hall. Alistair's head snapped round, but there was absolutely nothing between him and Diana and the locked doors. The footsteps headed straight towards the two of them. Alistair decided he was damned if he was going to give way. He shot a quick glance at Diana. She seemed far more angry than scared, as she raked her gaze back and forth across the empty space. The footsteps stopped again.

'There's nothing there!' said Diana. 'What the hell is going on?'

'I don't believe any of this,' Alistair said flatly. 'It's like your theatrical stories – too dramatic to be real.'

'But we all heard the footsteps! Where were they coming from?'

'Beats the hell out of me,' said Alistair. 'Want to go over to the doors and take a look?'

She shot him a startled glance, followed by a brave smile. 'Not really, no. But I will if you will.'

'It's just like facing a new congregation,' said Alistair. 'Never let them know you're scared.'

He started forward, and was quietly pleased to find Diana was right there with him. And then they both stopped abruptly as a new set of footsteps started. Only this time they seemed to be walking across the ceiling, passing right through the rows of tube lights as though they weren't there. Alistair craned his head right back, and still couldn't see anything. He heard more footsteps, and looked quickly round to find June and Leslie hurrying over to join them. There was something reassuringly solid and ordinary about the sounds they made. June looked furious, while Leslie looked baffled.

'Can you hear that?' said June, pointing at the ceiling.

'How could we not?' said Diana, doing her best to sound calm and assured. 'Someone's got their boots on.'

'What the hell are they doing on the ceiling?' said Leslie.

Alistair looked sternly at June. 'Did you arrange this?'

'Of course not!' She wrenched her eyes away from the ceiling to shoot him a somewhat guilty look. 'All right, yes; we had a few things set up for later . . . Just in case you people needed a little prompting . . . but nothing like this!'

Alistair turned to Leslie. 'Can you see anything?'

He shook his head slowly. 'No . . . But I can feel a presence. Something very old, and very angry.'

Alistair stared up at the ceiling. He simply couldn't bring himself to accept that the footsteps were in any way real. There was something almost arrogant about the sounds, as though they were rubbing his nose in their existence and defying him not to believe what was happening. And then the footsteps stopped. It was suddenly very quiet in the hall. Leslie took a deep breath and moved slowly forward, one step at a time.

He held one hand out before him, like a blind man feeling his way, and then stumbled to a halt.

'What is it?' said June.

'It's cold!' said Leslie. Suddenly he was shivering and hugging himself. 'I think it's an actual cold spot. Can't you feel it?'

Alistair and Diana looked at each other and shook their heads. June moved hesitantly forward to join Leslie, and then she started shivering too.

'Damn, that's cold! It's freezing!'

'I know!' said Leslie.

Alistair started forward, and Diana went with him. They'd only managed a few steps when the side door slammed open. They all jumped and turned to look, as Indira came striding into the hall.

'What the hell is going on?' she said loudly. 'None of the ovens will work, and I can't do a thing with them!'

They all jumped again as Toby came striding through the side door, scowling all over his face.

'The light just went out in the toilet! I nearly caught myself in my zip! What is wrong with this place?'

Alistair looked at Diana. 'That . . . is a very good question.'

THREE
Telling Stories in the Dark

I t didn't take Toby and Indira long to realize they'd missed something. They looked from face to face, taking in the general expressions of shock and awe, and then looked quickly round the empty hall.

'All right,' said Toby. 'What the hell happened, while we were otherwise occupied? Ghosties and ghoulies line-dancing on the stage, or spirits from the vasty deep offering free time-sharing vacations in the hereafter?'

'Not exactly,' said Diana.

'Something did happen though, didn't it?' said Indira. 'Something that proved we're not alone here . . .'

Alistair took it on himself to talk them through the experience, from the first footsteps in the shadows to the uncanny stroll across the ceiling; but he could tell he wasn't getting across just how otherworldly the whole thing had seemed. Toby looked stubbornly unconvinced, while Indira just looked increasingly confused.

'What's so scary about a few footsteps?' Toby said finally. 'It's just some odd noises, which is only what you'd expect from a building this old. It's not like you were in any danger.'

'You had to be there, darling,' said Diana. 'And you weren't.'

Toby bristled at the suggestion that this was somehow his fault, but Alistair could tell from Indira's wide eyes that she was perfectly happy to have missed out. She stared quickly back and forth, trying to pierce the darker shadows with her unsettled gaze, as though half expecting the spiritual sounds to show up again at any moment.

'I didn't hear anything in the kitchen,' she said. 'If the footsteps were as loud as you're suggesting, why didn't I hear anything?'

'The sounds were very localized,' said Alistair. 'And they seemed to head straight for us. Almost as though we were being targeted.'

'OK . . .' said Toby, 'that didn't sound at all paranoid.' He looked at June and Leslie. 'You're being very quiet, for a change. Don't you have anything to say? You're supposed to be the experts.'

'We didn't expect anything like what just happened,' said June, in a surprisingly subdued voice. 'It was just noises. I'm not sure they mean anything.'

'It could have been some kind of message,' said Leslie. 'Or possibly a warning.'

'Telling us what?' Diana said sharply. 'That we should get the hell out of the hall? What use is that, when we're trapped in here?'

'Would ghosts understand the situation?' said Alistair, trying to sound honestly interested and not just sarcastic.

'You tell us,' said Toby. 'You're the expert on the hereafter.'

'But . . . what if we had to leave?' said Indira, her voice shaking unhappily. 'What if things became so dangerous we couldn't stay here? What would we do then?'

Her voice was rising by the end, tinged with hysteria. Toby stopped trying to disparage what had happened, and moved in beside Indira, trying to calm her with his presence. She didn't even seem to realize he was there.

'Can we all please hang on to our common sense!' June said loudly. 'It was just some sounds!'

Alistair looked at her thoughtfully. 'Is there anything about phantom footsteps in the local stories?'

June looked at him blankly. 'Didn't you even bother to read the background information pack we sent you? It had details on all the ghost stories.'

'I never got anything like that,' said Alistair. He looked at the other guests, and they all shook their heads.

June looked as if she wanted to spit fire and call down the lightning.

'Did nobody on·the support team do what they were supposed to? I spent ages putting those information packs together, in plenty of time to get them out to the guests! But then, why should that have gone right when nothing else has? Once this show is over, an awful lot of people are going to be looking for new jobs, and just maybe some of their internal organs!'

'A lot of those people have already left,' said Leslie. 'Rats, deserting a sinking ship.'

June glared at him. 'Really not helping.'

'You still haven't answered my question,' said Alistair, as politely as he could because he didn't want to trigger another outburst.

June stared at him for a moment, as though she couldn't remember why he was there, and then struggled to pull her professional calm around her.

'I can't remember any story off-hand that included phantom footsteps. What about you, Leslie? You're the one who's interested in all that supernatural crap.'

Leslie was already shaking his head. 'Lots of local people talked about hearing strange noises inside the hall when it was supposed to be empty, but I don't recall anyone mentioning footsteps.'

'I'm more interested in where they were going, and why,' said Diana. 'I mean, they all walked in straight lines, as though they were heading somewhere specific.'

'Maybe they were just trying to get the hell out of here,' said Toby. 'Which is entirely understandable. I've only just arrived, and I can't wait to see the back of this place.'

'Whoever they were, they moved slowly and with purpose,' said Diana. 'Like they had business with us . . .'

'Like they wanted to hurt you?' said Indira. 'Or like they wanted to take you away . . .'

Her voice was starting to rise again. Alistair decided that yet again it was down to him to be the voice of reason, because no one else seemed interested in the position.

'We can't be sure they were footsteps,' he said firmly.

'What do you mean?' Diana said immediately. 'We all heard them.'

'We heard noises,' Alistair said firmly. 'Which we interpreted as footsteps, because they continued in a regular progression.

But really they were just a bunch of separate sounds, coming one after the other. I think what we were hearing might just have been old wood, expanding and contracting. Delayed echoes of our own footsteps, vibrating through the wooden floorboards. Remember, the sounds didn't start until after we'd been walking around here for a while.'

One by one heads started to nod, as the group considered the idea and decided they could live with it. Indira actually relaxed a little, and started to smile.

'Nicely reasoned, Bishop,' said June. 'But in the future, please keep that kind of rational explanation to yourself. We are in the ghost business, so from now on I want anything that happens interpreted as unquiet spirits or dead men walking; because that's what the audience at home wants. If the sounds start up again, concentrate on good reactions and witty remarks. A little humour always helps the horror go down.'

Toby glared at her. 'I came on this show to be a celebrity guest, not a puppet.'

'When I pull your strings, you'd better dance,' June said flatly. 'Or I will kick your arse until you do.'

'She really would,' Leslie said solemnly. 'I've seen her do it.'

'Wouldn't surprise me one bit, darling,' said Diana.

'Will you all please calm the hell down!' said June. 'Honestly, it's like working with a bunch of kids straight from stage school. We had a great opportunity to make use of those sounds, but we blew it by being caught off guard. I don't want that to happen again.'

Alistair looked at her thoughtfully. 'Why did those noises throw you so badly? I would have thought you and Leslie had enough experience in these matters to cope with anything the hall could throw at you.'

June and Leslie exchanged a quick look, and something passed between them that Alistair could see but not quite grasp.

'We're not used to anything happening,' said Leslie.

Alistair frowned. 'Are you saying you have no experience when it comes to otherworldly phenomena?'

'Of course not!' said June. 'We didn't come here to hunt ghosts, just to look as though we are.'

The guests stared at each other, and Alistair took the moment to study them all carefully. Toby was frowning, Indira was still trying to decide how she felt, and Diana was concealing her true feelings behind a professional mask. She straightened her back, raised her chin, and smiled brightly at June.

'So, what do you want us to do now?'

'Act normally,' Leslie said carefully. 'This is the point where we would demonstrate the various kinds of ghost-hunting equipment we provide, so you can get some practice in how to use them. There should be a table covered in the things . . . but, as you can see, they're not here.'

'Bloody stage crew!' said June. 'What is wrong with everyone on this show?'

'Maybe you're being sabotaged,' said Toby.

The words seemed to hang on the air. Everyone looked at Toby, and he shrugged quickly.

'Well, think about it. Could one of the other ghost-hunting shows have bribed some of your people to put the boot in while you're down, so there'd be one less show fighting for the diminishing audience share?'

June actually brightened at the thought, but Leslie shook his head firmly.

'We're no longer big enough to be a threat to anyone. Why would the other production companies put themselves at risk, when all they have to do is stand back and wait for us to fail?'

'We are not going to fail!' said June. 'We've got the perfect high concept in the perfect setting, and if everyone will just do their damned job, we will put on a show so heart-stoppingly terrifying that people will be talking about it for years!'

She glared around at her guests, and they glared right back at her, irked at the suggestion that they hadn't been pulling their weight. Alistair decided once again that it was his job to calm things down.

'What kind of scientific equipment do you normally provide?'

'The usual,' said Leslie. 'Motion trackers, thermal scanners, and electro-magnetic displays. They all come with blinking lights, glowing screens, and impressive sound systems. We get free samples from all the big companies, as long as we mention their names on air.'

'Do any of them really do anything?' said Diana, in a voice that suggested she already knew the answer.

'Well, yes and no,' said Leslie. 'These instruments were designed to measure real-world phenomena, not spiritual presences. We only use them for dramatic purposes. Nothing like a good prop to raise someone's performance.'

'There's nothing more riveting than watching someone follow a motion tracker into the dark,' June said fondly. 'Or read off the dropping temperature on a thermal scanner. That can really put the wind up an audience.' A thought struck her, and she looked quickly at Toby and Indira. 'I don't suppose you happened to see any of our little toys when you were out the back?'

'The kitchens are a mess,' Indira said flatly. 'Hardly anything there, and what there was didn't work.'

'And I definitely didn't see any kind of high tech in the toilet,' said Toby. 'Unless you count the flush, where you have to wave your hand to make it work. That scanner really didn't want to cooperate. I had to wiggle my fingers like Doctor Strange before anything happened.'

'We could take a look in the storeroom at some point,' said Leslie. 'But I can't see any reason why the crew would have put them there.'

'Have you been able to depend on your people, in the past?' said Alistair.

June's scowl darkened, and Leslie cut in quickly.

'We had to let the old crew go. We couldn't afford them. It's the same with Derek; he's a first-time director, taking a cut in pay in return for a step up the ladder. He brought his own people with him, as part of the package.'

'He promised me they were reliable!' said June. 'I should have had my suspicions when I saw how little we were getting them for.'

Alistair couldn't help noticing that June's hands had clenched into fists, and that she looked ready to use them. He also noticed that Leslie was watching her carefully. Alistair decided it was time for another distracting question.

'Didn't you have a backup plan in place? Just in case things went wrong?'

'Of course!' said June. 'But they depended on my being able to give the director instructions on my phone! God alone knows what kind of decisions he's been making on his own.'

'The phones should be working,' said Leslie. 'I can't see any good reason why they aren't. It's as though someone wants us cut off. Someone . . . or something.'

June gave him a hard look. 'Don't start . . .'

'So!' Diana said brightly. 'What's the plan?'

June did her best to appear the complete professional, and smiled determinedly round the group.

'We still have some time before we need to start the real action. When you're pulling an all-nighter, you don't want to peak too soon and lose your audience. We shouldn't show them anything too impressive until after twelve.'

'Midnight,' said Leslie, just a bit sepulchrally. 'The witching hour, when graves break open and the dead walk the night . . .'

June rose above him. 'There are sleeping bags and folding chairs for everyone, in the storeroom next to the kitchen. Or at least, there had bloody well better be, or gonads will roll. I suggest we get everything out and set up a nice little camp right here, in the middle of the hall. Then we can make ourselves comfortable and have a nice little chat. Get to know each other. It helps if the audience takes to the guests and feels involved with them; particularly when we seem to be putting you in danger later on.'

'Seem?' said Toby.

'You'll be perfectly safe!' said June. 'Except possibly from me.'

'We can also use the time to work out some entertaining bits of business to catch the audience's eye,' Leslie said quickly. 'Like a nice confessions chat later. Baring the soul always goes down well on a ghost show.'

'So you're not interested in spontaneous reactions?' said Alistair.

'Of course not,' said June.

'Trust us,' said Leslie. 'We've gone through seven series of this show, and three specials. We know what works and what doesn't.'

'If everyone just acts naturally, they end up bumping into each other, and talking over everyone's best lines,' said June. 'What we need is the appearance of spontaneity, so we can milk it for all it's worth.'

'She's not wrong,' said Diana. 'First thing you learn in the theatre is that the appearance of spontaneity takes a lot of rehearsing.'

'I feel like a child discovering there's no Santa Claus,' said Toby.

'I never did believe in him,' said Alistair.

Diana raised a painted eyebrow. 'You believe in an invisible friend in the sky, but you draw the line at Santa Claus?'

Alistair smiled easily. 'When I was a kid, my dad used to run a small toy shop, so I always knew where everyone's presents came from. Every Christmas Eve, the whole family would have to help out in the shop, to deal with the extra business; and when we were done we'd lock the doors, smile at the empty shelves, and sing a quick chorus of "What a friend we have in Jesus".'

Diana stared at him, honestly shocked. 'Bish, really!'

'You must see a lot of things, backstage in your church,' Toby said slowly. 'Don't they undermine your faith?'

'Faith isn't faith if it falls apart when you test it,' said Alistair.

Diana glanced at the hidden wall cameras. 'Getting to know each other sounds fun, darlings, but I'm not prepared to bare my soul.'

'As opposed to your teddy bear?' said Toby, wriggling his eyebrows suggestively.

'That was different,' Diana said coldly. 'A star needs to maintain a sense of mystery.'

'Think of it as appearing on a chat show,' said June. 'No one expects you to tell the truth; just roll out your best anecdotes.'

'And if anyone should start saying things the audience

doesn't need to know,' said Leslie, 'the director can cut the mikes and play some spooky music. One of the first things everyone in our line of work learned from the Big Brother-type shows is that audiences want the illusion of live television, not the real thing. Most conversation is boring, self-serving, or embarrassing. Much better to concentrate on the best bits, and work hard at maintaining the right mood.'

'The more I learn about how this show works,' said Alistair, 'the more cynical I feel.'

'Welcome to the world of entertainment,' said Toby. 'Depressing, isn't it?'

'I'm a professional actress,' said Diana. 'And I still feel a little bit shocked. If you can't believe in live television, what can you believe in?'

Alistair smiled at her. 'See me afterwards.'

Toby took it on himself to get things moving, like a master of ceremonies at a holiday camp. He clapped his hands together and smiled brightly about him.

'Chairs and sleeping bags sound like a really good idea to me. We've been standing around for far too long.'

'Damn right,' said Diana. 'My feet are killing me.'

'I'm not surprised, with those stilettos,' said Toby. 'Those heels are so high you could stab someone to death.'

'Don't tempt me,' said Diana.

Indira looked steadily at Toby. 'You did have a good idea, earlier. I think we could all use a nice cup of tea. But I don't want to go back into the kitchen on my own.'

Toby started to crack a joke, but stopped when he realized she was serious. He smiled reassuringly at her.

'Don't worry about it. I'll go with you, and keep you company.'

'And while you're doing that, Diana and I will retrieve the sleeping bags and chairs from the storeroom,' said Alistair.

'Thanks for volunteering me, darling,' said Diana.

'I knew you wouldn't mind,' said Alistair.

'I can show you where everything is,' said June.

'I'm staying here,' said Leslie.

They all looked at him.

'On your own?' said Diana.

'I don't think I'll come to any harm,' said Leslie. 'After everything that's happened, I need to listen to the hall and see what it has to say to me.'

June sniffed. 'You are such a drama queen.'

Leslie raised an eyebrow. 'Isn't that what you pay me for, on this show?'

Toby started toward the side door, and then stopped as he realized Indira hadn't moved. She was still staring at the door like a mouse confronted by a snake. Toby moved carefully to block her view.

'I'll go in first. You just follow on behind.'

He started forward again, and this time Indira went with him. Toby shouldered open the door, as though daring anything to get in his way, and the two of them disappeared.

'I'm pleased to see Toby coming out of his shell, and acting so protectively towards Indira,' Alistair said to Diana. 'Though why he chose to take her under his wing . . .'

'I think it's very sweet,' said Diana.

Alistair looked at her. 'What is?'

Diana patted him fondly on the cheek. 'I'm sure it'll come to you.'

'If you two have quite finished gossiping,' June said loudly, 'there's work that needs doing.'

'After you, fearless leader,' said Diana.

June led them over to the side door, and Alistair and Diana followed her through. The light in the cramped little foyer beyond the side door consisted of a single bare bulb. Alistair glanced through the open kitchen door, where Toby and Indira were chatting cheerfully as they sorted out the tea things, and then looked thoughtfully at the single toilet door.

'Don't you believe in unisex toilets, Bish?' said Diana.

'I suspect this one had less to do with forward-thinking, and more to do with saving money,' said Alistair.

June made an impatient noise to attract their attention, and pushed open the door to the storeroom. It turned out to be more of a closet with delusions of grandeur, and when June tried the light switch, nothing happened. June started to swear, and then glanced at Alistair and stopped herself. He smiled easily.

'Don't mind me. Most of my parishioners would be hard pressed to come up with any word that had more than four letters in it.'

'Do you swear?' said Diana. She sounded honestly curious.

'Oh yes,' said Alistair. 'But I do it in Latin, so nobody knows.'

'Sneaky,' said Diana. 'I like it.'

In the end, June had to hold the storeroom door open so the light could get in, while Alistair and Diana took it in turns to haul out the rolled-up sleeping bags, drag them into the main hall, and dump them there. Alistair paused for a moment, and then drew Diana's attention to Leslie. The medium was standing deep in the shadows, staring at nothing. Diana sniffed.

'He's not fooling anyone but himself.'

They went back for more sleeping bags. Once they'd finished, June gestured at the folding chairs. Alistair and Diana stood their ground and looked at her meaningfully, until she got the message and helped them carry the chairs into the main hall. Once it was all done, Alistair straightened up slowly and massaged his aching back muscles with both hands.

'Oh I know, darling,' said Diana, stretching languorously. 'I normally have people to do this sort of thing for me.'

'Fans?' said Alistair.

'Oh please,' said Diana. 'Like I'd let them get anywhere near me. Never encourage fans, it gives them ideas.'

Alistair turned to June. 'What would you have done, if the sleeping bags and chairs hadn't been there?'

'Fired a whole bunch of people, for starters,' June said flatly.

She organized Alistair and Diana into unrolling the sleeping bags and laying them out in a circle, with a chair set in place beside each bag. Alistair considered the layout and decided it looked rather cosy. Diana wasn't so sure, and didn't care who knew it. She glowered at the sleeping bags, and then fixed June with her best hard stare.

'You don't really believe any of us are going to get a wink of sleep in this place?'

'You'd be surprised,' said June. 'It's going to be a long night, and people can get really tired jumping at shadows.'

And then she paused, and shot Diana a sideways look. 'Or are you worried the footsteps might return while you're sleeping, and trample you?'

'Wouldn't be the first time someone in this business walked all over me,' Diana said coldly.

Alistair left them to it, and walked over to the edge of the shadows so he could look at Leslie. The medium had his hands clasped together before his chest, and his head lowered, as though lost in prayer. Or perhaps he was just listening. Diana broke off her skirmishing with June and came over to stand beside Alistair. She leaned in close so she could lower her voice.

'What do you suppose he's doing?'

'I think those unexpected footsteps affected him more than he'll admit,' said Alistair. 'June was very emphatic that neither of them had ever encountered actual phenomena before.'

'But that could be just what they want us to think,' Diana said wisely. 'Always remember: those two are performers, first and foremost.'

'But if Leslie really is feeling disturbed, it's my duty to help him,' said Alistair. 'So if you'll excuse me for a moment . . .'

'Don't let me stop you, darling.'

Alistair walked into the shadows until he was standing next to Leslie. It felt like walking on the bottom of the sea, where all the dead things end up. The medium didn't even glance at Alistair.

'Are you picking up anything?' Alistair said politely.

'You don't believe in mediums,' said Leslie.

'I don't disbelieve,' Alistair said carefully. 'I don't know enough about the subject. I try to keep an open mind.'

'That's the last thing you should do,' said Leslie. 'You can never tell what might walk in.' He turned his head suddenly, to fix Alistair with a steady gaze. 'Would you pray for my soul, if I died?'

Alistair looked at him, but treated the question seriously. 'Of course.'

'Then I will pray for yours,' said Leslie.

He turned abruptly, and strode back out of the shadows. He

trampled across the sleeping bags, chose a chair, and sat down, all without once glancing at June. Who didn't seem to give a damn what the medium did. Alistair took his time walking back out of the shadows, because he didn't want anyone thinking they might be bothering him. Diana made her way into the circle of sleeping bags, as though she didn't have a care in the world. It was a good performance, and would have fooled anyone who hadn't spotted the tension in her back and shoulders. She dropped into the nearest chair, and crossed her long legs with casual grace. Only the slightest quiver in her raised foot gave her away. Alistair pretended not to have noticed. Diana gestured for him to come and sit beside her, so he did. She inclined her head toward him, and lowered her voice again.

'I'm starting to think we're the only level-headed ones in this group. June and Leslie have their own agenda, Indira's only just holding herself together, and Toby is only interested in looking after her. So, you and I need to stick together.'

'I have no problem with that,' said Alistair.

She smiled at him, and relaxed a little. 'You know, you're a very comforting person, Bish.'

'It's all part of the job.'

'I never really thought about ghosts, one way or the other,' Diana said slowly. 'Except in stories. But now I'm not sure what I believe.'

'Believe in yourself,' said Alistair. 'And your good sense.'

'What do you believe, right now?'

'That there's more going on here than meets the eye,' said Alistair.

'Would you stand between me and a ghost?' said Diana.

'Of course,' said Alistair. 'Though it would probably walk right through me.'

They shared a smile. Their hands moved together, and might have clasped, but the two of them got distracted as June dropped heavily into a chair beside Leslie. She glowered at the medium, but he wouldn't even look in her direction.

'Go on then,' said June. 'Sulk. See how far that gets you.'

Leslie folded his arms tightly and shook his head. 'I don't want to do this.'

'You agreed. You agreed it was necessary.'

'Yes,' said Leslie. 'I did, didn't I?'

The side door opened, and Toby held it back so Indira could carry out a battered tin tray bearing assorted mugs of steaming tea. They joined the others in the circle, and Toby smiled proudly round at everyone.

'I want it understood by one and all that I made this tea! I found the tea bags at the back of a cupboard, I boiled the water, dropped the tea bags into the mugs, and poured on the water. All while keeping up a steady patter of amusing conversation.'

'It's true,' said Indira. 'He wouldn't let me do anything.'

'And now for the bad news,' said Toby. 'There wasn't any milk or sugar, so you'll just have to take it basic black.'

'I did find a packet of biscuits,' said Indira. 'But they were so old you could have dunked them for an hour without softening them.'

'I suggested we use them as coasters,' said Toby. 'But Indira didn't like the way they twitched when they thought no one was looking.'

Indira giggled cheerfully. Her time in the kitchen with Toby seemed to have restored some of her self-confidence.

'The tea is nice and hot,' she said brightly. 'So get it down you.'

She passed the tray around so everyone could grab a mug, and then she and Toby sat down on the two remaining seats, completing the circle. Alistair warmed his hands on his mug, and sipped the tea carefully. He didn't pull a face. Enduring all kinds of tea was just part of his duties when he made the rounds of his parish. And he did find the tea soothing, as a familiar ritual in an uneasy setting. The group sat quietly together, heads bent over their mugs, considering how to talk about things they weren't sure they wanted to talk about.

'At least the spooky footsteps haven't returned,' Diana said finally.

'You had to bring that up, didn't you?' said Toby. 'That's almost as bad as saying *What could possibly go wrong?*'

'I'm not hearing any supernatural sounds now,' said Indira,

staring past the people sitting opposite her so she could keep a wary eye on the shadows.

Alistair could see her hands trembling around her mug. Toby saw it too, and moved quickly to distract Indira with a new story.

'Not that long ago, I saw a ghost in my bedroom,' he said. 'I was lying in bed when a ghost walked through my window and into the room. It started toward me, but I wasn't scared, just furious at the intrusion. So I jumped out of bed to punch the ghost in the face. And of course that's when I woke up, and realized it was just a dream. Never be afraid of ghosts, Indira; it's much better to make them afraid of you.'

'I don't think I could actually hit one,' said Indira, though her expression suggested she was seriously considering it.

'You can always call for me,' said Toby. 'And I will kick its ectoplasmic arse all over the place.'

Indira smiled. 'I would like to see that.'

'I'm not sure how it would appear on camera,' said Toby. 'Me with one foot in the air, trying to kick nothing at all. Probably end up flat on my back.'

Indira bent her head over her mug to hide a giggle.

'We are not expecting to encounter any ghosts,' June said firmly. 'All you need to do is act as though you're seeing something, so we can give the little sensation-seekers their money's worth. And don't let this place get to you. It's all too easy for your imagination to run out of control, when you're deep in the mood and the adrenalin's racing.'

'It might help if we were to discuss what a ghost really is,' said Alistair.

'Good idea,' said Diana. 'After you.'

'Go for it,' said June. 'I'm sure our audience would be fascinated to learn what a man of the cloth has to say on the subject. But keep it brief and to the point; we're not dealing with long attention spans here.'

Alistair leaned forward, choosing his words carefully. 'People have been seeing ghosts throughout recorded history. That wise old historian, Pliny the Elder, wrote a long piece about a haunted villa in ancient Rome. So you can't say that people don't see ghosts, because they do. What we can, and should, be discussing is exactly what it is they're seeing.

'There are all kinds of theories. There's the traditional belief that ghosts and spirits are the conscious remains of a living person, unable to move on. Trapped, perhaps, by old memories or unfinished business, or because they're not ready to give up the lives they knew. Other people believe that ghosts are simply memories from the past. That some experiences are so intense they soak into their surroundings and play back later. Like a stone tape.'

'But what do you believe?' said Diana.

'I think when it's time for us to go, we go,' said Alistair. 'Because there's a better place prepared for us.'

'Then what do you think a ghost is?' said Indira, peering owlishly over her mug.

'Perhaps the spiritual equivalent of a message in a bottle,' said Alistair. 'Something left behind.'

'You've given the matter a lot of thought,' said Diana.

'Comes with the territory,' said Alistair.

Diana turned to June. 'Have you really never run into anything that could pass for a ghost, in all the time you've been doing this?'

'Not once,' said June. 'I never expected to, and never wanted to, because it would only have got in the way of putting on a good show.'

'And there's nothing like having your show under threat of being cancelled by know-nothing executives, to convince you that there's no life after death,' said Leslie. 'Or at least, nothing you can live with.'

'What about the people who watch your show because they believe in ghosts?' said Toby.

'They get their beliefs corroborated,' said June. 'And a chance to say "I told you so" to their disbelieving friends.'

'And the viewers who don't believe?' said Diana.

'They get to watch the show in a spirit of irony,' said June. 'And feel superior to their friends who do believe. So we get them coming and going: a perfect win-win situation.'

'But what do shows like yours do for people who believe in the scientific investigation of ghosts?' said Alistair.

'Screw them,' said June. 'Let them get their own show, if they can. The public doesn't have much time for ghost-hunters who can't provide the goods on demand.'

'The idea of using science to investigate the supernatural has always seemed ridiculous to me anyway,' said Leslie. 'That's like calling in a vet because someone's told you about a headless dog.'

'A dog with no head?' said Toby, grinning broadly. 'How does it smell?'

Indira collapsed into serious giggles, and slapped his shoulder. Toby looked quietly proud. Diana kept her attention fixed on June.

'But you were ready to use all the latest scientific toys.'

'Only for dramatic effect,' said June. 'Give an actor a prop to hold, and they're happy.'

'It's all just stage dressing,' said Leslie. 'Ghost-hunting scientists always remind me of butterfly collectors, chasing after things to put them on display. In the end, all they have is something that used to be free and beautiful, pinned to a board.'

'Someone should found a special society,' said Toby, just a bit grandly. 'Dedicated to protecting and preserving ghosts. Before they become endangered.'

'Maybe that's why so few people are seeing ghosts these days,' said Indira. 'Because they're hiding from us.'

'I told you,' said Toby. 'They're more afraid of us than we are of them.'

He toasted her with his mug, and she toasted him back.

Alistair looked round at everyone over the rim of his mug as he sipped his tea. They all seemed a lot more relaxed, now they'd talked through the subject. Which was why he'd brought up the idea in the first place. He surreptitiously studied the shadows surrounding the sleeping bags, and it seemed to him that they were deeper and darker than ever. He couldn't help feeling that something was going on in the hall that he didn't understand; something secret and dangerous.

June made a point of checking her watch. 'OK, people; we still have plenty of time before we need to start staring off camera and shouting, "What was that?" For now, I need you all to open up a little. Confession is good for the viewing figures. I'm not asking you to reveal any deep dark secrets; just a few juicy anecdotes that might or might not be true, to help the audience get a handle on you. They're always happiest when each guest has a clearly defined role.'

She looked round the circle, but no one seemed keen to go first.

'Am I going to have to point at someone?' said June, just a bit threateningly.

'Why don't you start, darling?' Diana said sweetly.

'Because I'm the host, and they already know me,' said June. 'Step up, people; it's time to sing for your supper. Come on, it's not that difficult. Start with . . . why you're here. What persuaded you to come on this show in the first place.'

'It certainly wasn't the money,' said Diana. 'I've been paid more for a personal appearance at a sewage works. Oh hell, I'll take the lead. I've done enough chat shows in my time. I am here to lend a touch of glamour to the proceedings, and give your audience someone worth looking at if the ghosts don't show up.'

'You've always been good at keeping yourself in the public eye,' said Toby. 'Like the nude photo with the teddy bear. But why pick a failing reality show like this? Do you really need the publicity that badly? You've had a long and successful career . . .'

'The key word there is *long*,' said Diana. 'I'm not as young as I used to be. The competition is baying at my heels; all those pretty young things fighting to get their first step on the ladder by dragging me down. More and more I'm having to fight for parts I used to take for granted, and every day I have to spend longer in front of the mirror to make myself look like me. Bottom line, darlings: any publicity is better than none.'

They all looked at her. No one had heard Diana be that serious for so long.

'But why choose this show, in particular?' said Alistair.

'I didn't,' said Diana. 'It was the only one that would have me.'

For a moment, Alistair thought he saw something tired and

trapped looking out of Diana's eyes, but then she pulled herself together and smiled determinedly at him.

'Tell us something about yourself, Bish. How did you get into religion?'

He smiled back at her. 'You make it sound like a career choice. I felt I had a calling, that this was what I was supposed to be doing with my life. People need someone to comfort and protect them, and help them see the bigger picture. It was either this . . . or be a social worker. And the church has better outfits.'

'But they made you Bishop of All Souls Hollow,' said Toby. 'I know that area; the part of London that civilization forgot. At night you can see Neanderthal men sitting outside abandoned warehouses, inventing fire. How do you cope?'

'By offering hope and help to those who need it,' said Alistair. 'God has a plan for all of us.'

Toby stared into his mug. 'You say that like it's a good thing.'

'I don't believe in God,' Diana said abruptly.

'That's all right,' said Alistair. 'She believes in you.'

A series of startled laughs ran around the circle.

'Oh, your superiors must just love you,' said Toby.

'Why do you think they stuck me on morning television?' said Alistair. 'What better way to defuse a potentially dangerous free-thinking trouble-maker than by making them a minor celebrity that no one takes seriously?' He thought for a moment. 'In the end, I think my faith comes from a need to believe that *somebody* cares. Because if they didn't, the world would be unbearable.'

There was a pause as June looked hard at Toby and Indira, willing them to volunteer. Toby stared defiantly back. And then, without looking up from her mug, Indira just started talking.

'I never expected to win that cooking contest,' she said quietly. 'I only applied because I thought it might be fun, and a chance to prove to my family that I could do something, and do it well. But once I'd won, I had to go on. Make a career for myself, with the opportunity that had been handed to me.'

'How did your family react, once you'd won the competition?' said Toby. 'Were they supportive?'

'They didn't care,' said Indira. 'They never have.' She finally raised her face, and looked through the people in the circle, concentrating on the shadows beyond them. 'I'm only here because I thought I could use this show to publicize my new book. I don't know what I would have done if I'd been here when you heard those footsteps. I'm afraid of ghosts. But then, I'm afraid of everything.'

'You don't have to be,' said Toby. 'I'm here. And I will stand between you and anything that might try to hurt you.'

Indira looked at him. 'Why would you do that?'

'Because there was no one to do it for me when I needed them,' said Toby.

Indira nodded slowly, and then looked back into her mug. June fixed her gaze on Toby in a way that said, *You're the only one left*. But still he didn't say anything.

'Why did you decide to be a stand-up comedian?' Alistair said finally. 'Did you feel a calling, like me?'

'Not really,' said Toby. 'At first, it was just a chance to get out of a job I hated. After I'd been hitting the clubs for a while, I honestly thought I had it in me to be a great comedian. It came hard to discover I was only good at it.'

Indira looked at him. 'But you're funny.'

'Not funny enough,' said Toby. He smiled suddenly. 'I admire your cooking skills, because I don't have any. I'm always on the road, heading from one venue to the next, which means I live on fast food and takeaways.'

Indira shook her head firmly. 'That's not a healthy way to live. It will catch up with you, one of these days.'

'It already has,' said Toby. 'I had my second heart attack four months ago. Stress and strain and a really bad diet will do that to you.'

Everyone sat up straight, half expecting it to be some kind of joke, but Toby's face didn't change.

'Should you be working again, so soon?' said Alistair.

'I have to,' said Toby. 'Stay off the circuit too long, and the audiences and the booking agents start to forget you.'

'Isn't it dangerous, for you to be in a stressful situation like this?' said Indira.

'It might be, if I believed in any of this crap,' said Toby. 'And anyway, I'm the guy who tried to punch a ghost, remember?'

A ripple of laughter ran round the circle, and Toby took advantage of the general openness to stare steadily at June and Leslie.

'What will you do, if this whole *Live Broadcast Special* thing doesn't work out? If you don't get your ratings back?'

'I'll end up back on the road, just like you,' said Leslie. 'Showing off my gifts to people who don't appreciate them.'

June sniffed loudly. 'I am a professional presenter. Which means I can sell anything, to anyone. I won't have any problem finding another job.'

She looked quickly round the group, as though challenging them to contradict her. Alistair wondered if she was trying to convince the group, or herself. Diana was already shaking her head.

'I used to have that kind of confidence, but it's amazing how fast people can get tired of your face.'

'Your face, maybe,' said June.

Everyone looked at her, and June seemed to realize she might have gone a little too far. She shot something that might have been an apologetic glance in Diana's direction, and quickly changed the subject.

'I never expected to have a career in ghosts. I took this job because it was offered, and the money was good. Somewhat to my surprise, I turned out to have a gift for persuading people that something supernatural was happening even when it blatantly obviously wasn't. And I am not giving it up! This show can still go all the way back to the top, if we all just work at it!'

'You always did think you could bully the world into seeing things your way,' said Leslie.

'Don't think you can slack off,' said June. 'You need this show.'

'So do you,' said Leslie. 'Like a junkie needs his fix.' He deliberately looked away from her, and smiled gently at the guests. 'If you've never watched this show, you've never seen me work. Would any of you like me to make contact with departed members of your families?'

The sudden question caught everyone off balance. They all glanced at each other, and then shook their heads firmly. Leslie didn't seem surprised by their reaction.

'You could at least have thought about it.'

'People get touchy when it comes to their loved ones,' said Alistair. 'Have you ever tried to contact someone from your own family?'

'No,' said Leslie. 'Because most of them are still very much a part of this vale of tears. And, dead or alive, none of them want to talk to me. My gift embarrasses the family. It always has.'

'But now you're famous . . .' said Toby.

'That just made it worse,' said Leslie. 'June was quite right. This show is all I have. The horror, the horror . . .'

Alistair looked quickly round the circle. It was clear people were starting to feel a little embarrassed at having rejected Leslie's offer so quickly. Alistair leaned forward on his chair, so he could face the man directly.

'But you still have faith in your abilities as a medium?'

'I have to,' said Leslie. 'Because the dead won't leave me alone.'

'You mean you hear voices?' said Indira.

'Only when I let them in,' said Leslie. He smiled easily round the circle. 'It's all right that you don't believe me. Unfortunately, I don't have any choice in the matter. It's not a matter of faith or belief, when the dearly departed are always trying to tap you on the shoulder.'

Alistair took another quick look round the circle. Nobody seemed to like that image much. They looked furtively at each other, hoping someone would change the subject.

Diana turned abruptly to face Alistair. 'I wish I had faith, like you, Bish.'

'You must believe in something,' said Alistair.

'I believe in the power of theatre,' said Diana. 'Telling stories that connect us all. When I know I've put in a good performance – that's when I feel most alive.'

'So it's not all about the applause, then?' said Toby. Indira tapped him lightly on the arm, and he hushed.

Alistair smiled encouragingly at Diana. 'How does your family feel, about you being a star?'

'They're all dead,' Diana said flatly. 'There's no one left but me. The theatre is my family.'

June made a point of checking her watch, and made a satisfied sound. 'It's finally past midnight. Time to get this show on the road.' She turned to Leslie, her expression stern and uncompromising. 'So put on the motley and go into your dance.'

Leslie peered doubtfully around the hall, and then nodded curtly. He rose to his feet and walked out of the circle and into the shadows. Alistair watched him carefully. Something about the man's calm but determined manner suggested a professional at work. Leslie finally settled on a spot that worked for him, and turned back to face the circle. He clasped his hands together and looked down at them. His face was hidden in the shadows. June smiled proudly round the group.

'He might be a pain in the arse, but he does put on a good show. Pay attention; you might learn something.'

Diana turned to Alistair. 'What's your position when it comes to mediums?'

'Just because the vast majority are undoubtedly crooks and scoundrels preying on the gullible and the emotionally vulnerable, it doesn't mean there couldn't be a few real talents,' Alistair said carefully. 'I just haven't met any yet. How about you?'

'Back during World War II, one of my great-aunts went to a medium,' said Diana. 'Her husband was serving in the Navy, and she wanted to be reassured he would come home safely. The medium said not to worry, he'd be fine. Two weeks later the telegram arrived, saying he'd been killed in action. And no one in my family had any time for mediums after that.'

'The medium was probably only trying to give your aunt some comfort,' said Alistair.

'Well, she didn't,' said Diana.

'I don't believe in mediums,' said Indira. 'I also don't believe the dead can come back to talk to the living. But just thinking about things like that is enough to scare me. If Leslie really can do all the things he says he can—'

'It's nothing but an act,' Toby said firmly. 'Like the cheery chappie persona I put on. Trust me: one fake can always recognize another.'

'I think Leslie is ready,' said June.

The medium walked slowly back out of the shadows and sat down facing the others. His back was straight, his head erect, and Alistair could feel the hackles stirring on the back of his neck as he took in the serene otherworldly expression on Leslie's face. June nodded knowingly to the group, as though to say, *Now you'll see something.* Leslie closed his eyes, took a deep breath, and cocked his head slightly to one side, as though listening to something only he could hear. His every movement was utterly compelling and convincing. And all around the circle, everyone watched him closely and held their breath.

When Leslie finally opened his eyes again, he stared right through the expectant faces before him. His head turned slowly back and forth, as though following the movements of some unseen crowd.

'Hello, my friends,' he said softly. 'Don't be afraid. Come to me, talk to me. You don't have to stay here if you don't want to. Let me help you on your way.'

'This is such bullshit,' Toby muttered.

Indira hushed him, watching Leslie with wide, fascinated eyes. As though she was afraid of what was happening, but more afraid to miss out on something. Leslie's lips continued to move, but no sound came from them, as though his words weren't intended for the living. Alistair glanced at Diana. She was concentrating on Leslie's every word and movement, like a drama critic determined not to be impressed. June nodded approvingly.

'This is what the audience wants. The full séance. Look at him go . . . This is why I keep him on. Because, for all his faults, the man does give good television.'

Alistair looked at Diana, and saw how tensely she was watching. He put a hand on her arm, and Diana's eyes snapped round to meet his.

'Are you feeling anything?' she said sharply.

'Not a thing,' Alistair said flatly. 'There's no one else here.'

Diana nodded slowly, and sat back on her chair, satisfied. 'Of course not. He's just an old pro, doing his job.'

'I feel like throwing something at him,' said Toby. 'Bet that would bring him out of his trance.'

'Don't you dare,' said Indira.

'You don't actually believe any of this nonsense?' said Toby.

'No. But I am interested.'

Leslie sat up straight in his chair, which creaked loudly at the movement and brought everyone's attention back to him.

'So many people . . .' he said. 'Going back so many years. This hall isn't just haunted; there are generations of the dead soaked into the wood and stone of this place.'

'All wonderfully vague,' said Diana. 'Nothing you could actually challenge him on.'

Alistair saw a quick frown come and go on June's face.

'That's enough stage setting,' she growled to Leslie. 'We need something big, to get this show off the ground. Talk to the man who died here recently. Albert Matheson; talk to him!'

Leslie didn't acknowledge her instructions, but he focused his gaze on one particular spot, as though concentrating on someone specific.

'Hello, Albert. Can you hear me? Albert . . .? I think he's confused. Not sure what happened to him, or where he is. Albert, you don't have to remain in this place. All your family and friends who have gone before are waiting for you to join them. Listen to my voice; I will help you find them.'

His voice was warm and compassionate, but Alistair was a little relieved to discover he wasn't in the least convinced. He glanced round at the other guests, and saw he wasn't alone in this. Diana was looking at Leslie with the utter contempt of one professional actor dismissing another. Toby looked like he was only moments away from some serious heckling. Even Indira seemed to have lost confidence in Leslie's performance. June glared at her guests and started to say something cutting, only to break off as Leslie made a sudden loud noise. His breathing became deep and harsh, and his body shook so hard it rocked the chair he was sitting on. And then suddenly he was sitting inhumanly still. Something had changed in his face. Alistair leaned forward despite himself, his skin crawling. There was a new tension on the air; a feeling of something about to happen. Diana's hand shot out to grab Alistair's, and he held it firmly.

'Did you feel that?' Diana said urgently. 'Something's happening . . .'

'There's something different about Leslie,' said Alistair. 'I think he's put himself in some kind of trance . . .'

'Someone has joined us,' said Leslie. He sounded calm, relaxed, almost amused. 'Don't anybody move, or leave the circle. This wouldn't be a good time to attract outside attention. There are forces at work here.'

'He's putting on a good show,' Toby said uncertainly. 'But that's all this is.'

'It's not a show any more,' said Indira.

'He is good,' said Diana, almost reluctantly.

'Not this good,' said June. 'I've never seen him like this.'

Alistair shot her a sharp look. She seemed honestly shaken, caught off balance by something she hadn't expected.

Indira stared at her. 'I thought you worked all this stuff out in advance?'

'Not this,' said June.

The medium turned his head slowly to look at Diana.

'You asked me earlier about your aunt, Felicia. She says . . . When you get home, look in the bottom drawer of your bureau. She left something there for you.'

Diana jumped as though she'd been hit. Her face was suddenly very pale, and her mouth trembled for a moment before she could regain her self-control.

'You don't know my aunt. You don't know anything about her.'

Leslie smiled gently, and when he spoke again, a woman's voice emerged from his lips.

'It's all right, Bunny. I'm fine. Be happy.'

Diana made a low shocked sound, and shrank back on her chair. Alistair squeezed her hand.

'Did that mean something to you?'

'Felicia always called me Bunny,' Diana said numbly. 'She was the only one who did. How could he know that?'

'Professional mediums always research the people they're going to work with,' said Alistair. 'Could you have mentioned your aunt before, in some old interview?'

'I don't know . . . Maybe.' Diana didn't sound at all convinced.

Leslie turned to Indira. 'Your father is here. He says he is very proud of you.'

Indira shook her head firmly. 'He would never say such a thing.'

'Not while he was alive,' said Leslie. 'But he sees things much more clearly now.'

'No!' Indira stood up abruptly, and Toby stood up with her. Indira glared at the medium, anger and outrage giving her a strength and intensity she hadn't possessed before. 'Stop this! I don't believe in you!'

And then she sat down again, staring at the ground so she wouldn't have to look at the medium. Toby stayed on his feet, glaring at Leslie.

'Cut the crap, right now.'

Leslie turned his head slowly, to smile at him. 'How's your heart, Toby? Any more of those chest pains?'

Toby started forward, but Indira grabbed his arm with both hands and pulled him down on to his chair. Leslie took a deep breath, and let it out slowly. The otherworldly look faded from his face, and he looked like himself again. He stretched unself-consciously. June was already on her feet and moving toward him. She leaned in close and muttered fiercely in his ear.

Diana looked down, realized she was still holding Alistair's hand, and jerked it free.

'It's all just research and theatrics,' said Alistair. 'You of all people should recognize that.'

'Yes, I should,' said Diana. 'But I'm not sure that's all that was.'

Toby leaned in close to Indira. 'Why did that thing about your father upset you so much?'

'Because I wanted it to be true,' said Indira. 'He always said . . . I was one daughter too many.'

'I would have been proud to be your father,' said Toby.
Indira's chest hitched. She looked like she was about to cry.
Toby put an arm across her shoulders, and she turned suddenly
and buried her face in his chest.

Leslie looked thoughtfully at June. 'I haven't been able to
make contact that easily in years.'

June shook her head. 'You picked a fine time to come out
of retirement.'

FOUR
Dead to the World

Leslie seemed honestly surprised to find that the whole group was staring at him, and not in a good way. He looked quickly around the hall, searching for some clue as to what might have happened, and then turned reluctantly back. June hit him with her hardest stare.

'What the hell was that all about?'

'What was what all about?' said Leslie. 'Did I start speaking in tongues or something?'

'It was definitely something,' said Toby. 'The folks at home must have been going out of their minds.'

'All right, it made for good viewing,' said June. 'But it wasn't what we'd agreed on!'

'You mean you and Leslie have been following a script, after all?' said Diana. 'I am shocked, I tell you, shocked.'

Leslie frowned. 'I can't seem to remember what happened, after I went into my trance. Did I say something wrong?'

'Just forget it,' Indira said abruptly. 'Let it go.'

She turned her back on the medium and walked out of the circle. Toby went after her. Leslie looked at Diana, but she didn't want to look at him, so he turned to Alistair, who could only shrug. Leslie didn't even bother to look at June. Faced with rejection by the whole group, he seemed to shrink in on himself. Diana turned suddenly and walked off, while June made an exasperated sound and turned her back on the medium, standing stiffly with her arms tightly folded. Only Alistair stayed with Leslie, because it felt wrong to leave the man on his own when he was so obviously confused.

'I only ever wanted to help people,' Leslie said quietly.

'Same here,' said Alistair. 'But if that was easy, everyone would be doing it.'

Leslie managed a small smile. 'The power is strong in me

tonight, though I couldn't tell you why. You believe what I do is real, don't you?'

Alistair considered his answer carefully. 'I'm prepared to believe . . . that you believe.'

'Well,' said Leslie. 'That's something.'

June suddenly turned back to face him, ignoring Alistair completely so she could concentrate the full force of her glare on the medium.

'I don't want you running any more of this personal baggage bullshit with the guests. It never plays well on camera. So get a hold of yourself, and put your persona back on! I need you to look like you know what you're doing.'

'You're not used to something real happening,' Leslie said quietly. 'But sometimes, when I open the door . . . I have no idea what will come through.' He smiled briefly. 'You did say you wanted something from me that would make an impression.'

'Didn't we just have a long conversation about the perils of spontaneity? I need you to stick to what we agreed!'

'There's something here, in the hall,' Leslie said flatly. 'Something we didn't allow for . . .'

'Don't give me that crap,' said June. 'I've worked with you too long to be fooled by your tired old song-and-dance act.'

Leslie looked at her, his face full of a long-standing hurt. 'You never did believe in me.'

'Of course not,' said June. 'I know you too well.'

And then they both looked round sharply, as they realized Alistair was still standing there, listening. Their faces suddenly became professionally blank, to make it clear he wasn't going to get anything else from them. Alistair got the impression they were worried they might have revealed something, though he had no idea what that could have been. June looked quickly round the hall and raised her voice.

'Pay attention, people! It's time to get this show on the road.'

Diana, Toby and Indira came back, somewhat reluctantly. They didn't look like they gave much of a damn about the show any more. June hit them with her most charming smile, though Alistair had to wonder how much of that was for the audience.

'Turn those frowns upside down, people. We're going to have some fun now, as I lead you on a grand tour of the hall.'

Diana smiled knowingly at her fellow guests. 'What she means is that she's going to tell us a bunch of spooky stories, about all the weird stuff that's happened here. It's just a disguised infodump, really.'

June shrugged. 'It's background. It's got to go somewhere.'

'Should we take notes?' Alistair said politely.

'Oh, I doubt much of it will be real, darling,' said Diana. 'June just wants to get the audience so worked up they'll be jumping at shadows along with the rest of us, and shouting, "It's behind you!" at their television sets.'

June leaned in close, and dropped her voice to a murmur. Her professional smile disappeared so quickly it was like looking at a different person.

'Do as you're told. You're being paid good money for this.'

'Good money, but not great,' said Toby, fixing June with his own cold stare. 'We are definitely not being paid enough to put our lives at risk. After your medium's little break with reality, I don't think any of us feel like putting our lives in your hands.'

Indira nodded quickly. 'Leslie said this hall was packed with ghosts.'

'And you believed him?' said June. 'I expect that kind of gullibility from the audience, but not from you.'

Diana raised an eyebrow. 'He's your pet medium.'

'Because I'm the one who rescued him from the feeble dog-and-pony act he was dragging round the theatres,' said June. 'Asking if there was anyone in the audience whose name started with an R . . . I made him a part of this show so he could serve a purpose, but that's all. Isn't that right, Leslie?'

Everyone turned to look at the medium, but he had his back to them and was staring off into shadows; apparently still disturbed by an experience he didn't understand. Alistair was half convinced that Leslie's performance, and June's reaction to it, were just an act . . . to put the guests in the right frame of mind for whatever came next. But he couldn't be sure.

'I'm feeling much better now,' Leslie said over his shoulder.
'If anybody cares . . .'

'Then get your act together!' said June.

'Don't I always, when it matters?' said Leslie. He turned
around to face her, and raised a placating hand. 'Whatever
you say, June. As always. Just point me in the right direction,
wind me up and watch me go for it.'

'Well,' said June. 'That's more like it.' She turned a sharp
gaze on the group. 'All of you agreed to appear on this show
because you thought you could get something out of it. For
Toby, a chance to jump-start a career that had stopped going
anywhere. Indira, a chance to push your new book after the
first one got roasted in the reviews. Diana, a chance to prove
to everyone that you aren't too old for the good parts. And
Alistair . . . A chance to prove your beliefs are real. Because
you're not as sure about that as you used to be.'

She looked around the group, defying them to challenge
anything she'd said. None of them said anything. June smiled
radiantly.

'Let's get moving then, shall we?'

'Where are we supposed to go?' Toby said truculently. 'We
can see all of the hall from here, and there isn't a single thing
worth looking at.'

'But I can show you all the secret nooks and crannies that
you don't know about,' said June. 'I will reveal wonders you've
never dreamed of; chill your blood with tales beyond your
worst nightmares; and allow the audience to experience the
hall through your reactions. That's the point of having guests.'

'Lead on,' said Alistair. 'I'm sure we're all just dying to
see what mysteries the hall has to offer.'

'Speak for yourself,' said Toby.

'Don't anyone wander off,' June said darkly. 'This is not a
good place to get caught on your own.'

She might have made more of an impression with her dire
warning if it hadn't been so obviously aimed at the audience.
The guests remained resolutely unimpressed. Toby actually
rolled his eyes. June adopted a power pose: legs set wide, with
her fists planted on her hips for maximum effect. But Toby
was having none of it.

'If you want to go wandering around this low-rent horror house, you can do it on your own,' he said flatly. 'We'll stay here with Leslie, who's at least shown some interest in protecting us from the bad stuff.'

It was clear to Alistair that Toby thought he was calling June's bluff, but Alistair wasn't so sure. To him, the whole confrontation between June and Leslie had the feel of just another of their set pieces, specifically created to play to the cameras. A little human drama to hold the audience's attention. Alistair couldn't help feeling that they should go with June, if only because she might reveal more about what she was really up to.

To everyone's surprise, June didn't flare up at Toby's open defiance. Instead, she just took a step forward and lowered her voice again.

'If you don't follow my lead,' she said calmly, 'and help me put across this vitally important segment of the show . . . I will make sure that none of you get paid.'

The guests looked at each other. It never even occurred to them to challenge her threat. It was just the kind of thing she would do.

'I knew I should have insisted on getting paid in advance,' said Diana.

Toby sighed, and scowled at his shoes. Indira tugged at his sleeve.

'You're not actually going to bow down to her, are you?'

'I don't have any choice,' said Toby, not looking at her. 'I need the money.'

'Come on,' said Alistair. 'A quick stroll around the hall won't do us any harm.'

Diana frowned at him, not even trying to hide her disappointment. 'I wouldn't have thought you cared about the money.'

'It all goes to charity,' said Alistair. 'I can do a lot of good in All Souls Hollow with that kind of money.'

Diana smiled suddenly, her faith in him restored. 'Of course you can.'

Alistair nodded to June. 'It's your walking tour. Where do we start?'

'The side door,' said Leslie.

Everyone turned sharply to look at him. It had been so long since he'd said anything, they'd almost forgotten he was there.

'Why there?' said Toby. 'There's nothing beyond that door worth the seeing.'

'You didn't look closely enough,' said Leslie.

June gathered everyone up with her eyes, and then strode over to the side door like a brave explorer heading into uncharted territory. Everyone else filed after her, at their own pace. Indira leaned in close to Toby.

'What does she think she's doing?'

'She probably just wants to make some speeches to the cameras in a new setting,' said Toby. 'A chance to upset the groundlings and send shivers down their spines. Got to keep throwing those Christians to the lions . . .'

'Did you notice anything out of the ordinary, when you were out the back?' said Alistair.

'Only more muck and filth than I'm used to seeing in anything but a comedy club's dressing room,' said Toby. 'Though the state of the toilet did come as a bit of a shock. And I'm a man who lives alone and has no idea where his Toilet Duck is.'

June waited for everyone to join her in the foyer, and then barged through the kitchen door, gesturing imperiously for the others to keep up. The kitchen turned out to be so small that June ended up with her back pressed against the far wall as she addressed the group. Packed shoulder to shoulder, the guests filled the kitchen from wall to wall; walls that they were careful not to touch in case some of the accumulated grime jumped off the cracked tiles to infect them. Nothing in the kitchen appeared to have been cleaned in living memory, and the ovens and surfaces were so filthy that Alistair felt like putting a hand over his mouth and nose and breathing shallowly, just in case.

Diana cried out suddenly, and would have jumped back if there'd been enough room. Indira grabbed Toby's arm with both hands, and looked wide-eyed at Diana.

'What did you see? Was it a ghost?'

'Worse!' said Diana. 'A cockroach!'

Everyone stared at her. Diana drew herself up and glared right back at them.

'It crawled out from under that oven! So big it would have shrugged off a mousetrap.'

'Where is it now?' said Alistair.

'I don't know! It darted back under the oven.'

Indira leaned forward for a close look, and then recoiled.

'Cockroach!' she said loudly. 'Big cockroach! And I was going to cook in here!'

'It's only a bug!' said June. 'If it's stupid enough to show its face again, feel free to stamp on the thing.'

'They have special sites on the internet for people like you,' said Toby.

'And it doesn't surprise me one bit that you know all about them,' said June.

'People are strange,' said Diana. 'When I was starting out, I was offered work on some odd little videos. One company wanted me to put on a wedding gown, jump into a swimming pool, then get out and parade around in the sopping wet dress.'

Everyone waited, but apparently that was the end of the story.

'Did you do it?' said Toby. He sounded honestly curious.

'Certainly not,' said Diana. 'I am an actress. And anyway, the money was pitiful. Just as well . . . Once you've made it, you can never be sure what will turn up from your past to embarrass you.'

'I didn't think you did embarrassment,' said Alistair.

Diana smiled. 'I don't, but my fans do on my behalf.'

'We're getting distracted, people,' said June, in a tone that suggested she'd run out of what little patience she had. 'I need you all to take a good look at this kitchen.'

'I'm trying really hard not to,' said Diana. 'It's filthy . . .' She raised an eyebrow at Indira. 'Are you still thinking about producing one of your special meals in here?'

'Not unless I can scrub down all the surfaces with industrial-strength bleach,' said Indira. 'And then fumigate the place with a flame-thrower.'

'Hold it,' said Toby. 'Indira . . . Where are your shopping bags? Did you take them out of the kitchen?'

'I never got around to it,' said Indira. 'They should still be on the shelf.'

She pointed, as best she could in the packed crowd, and everyone looked; but the shelf was quite definitely empty. 'My special ingredients!' said Indira. 'Someone's taken them!'

'They can't just have disappeared,' said Diana. 'Or do you think the ghosts did it?'

'Why would ghosts want them?' said Alistair.

'The dead always have their own agenda,' said Leslie.

It wasn't until he spoke up that everyone realized the medium hadn't squeezed into the kitchen with the rest of them. He was standing outside the doorway, looking in, as though he preferred to observe the proceedings from a safe distance.

'Things do have a reputation for going missing, in the hall,' Leslie said easily.

'But why would ghosts want to steal shopping bags full of food?' said Diana.

'Why do ghosts do anything?' said Leslie.

Diana glared at him. 'I would have thought that was your area of expertise.'

'Maybe the ghosts are hungry . . .' said Toby.

And then he stopped, as he realized he didn't like the implications of what he'd just said. Neither did anyone else. June looked distinctly annoyed at having her big moment undermined, and scowled at Indira.

'You can look for your shopping bags later. Right now, I have some important otherworldly stories that our audience needs to hear.'

Everyone gave June their full attention, and she launched into her prepared material. Alistair thought she made a pretty good job of it, with flashing eyes and dramatic gestures, as she recounted a series of weird incidents associated with the kitchen. Alistair didn't believe any of them. All the stories had a polished quality, with none of the stumbling or repetition you'd expect from a real anecdote. June talked about dark figures who appeared and disappeared in front of impeccable witnesses, or walked through walls as though they weren't there. Stories so simple and generic she probably got them

out of a *Big Book of Ghost Stories* she'd picked up at an
Oxfam shop. These were traditional stories, that had been told
so often all the details had rubbed off. But Alistair had to
admit that June did know how to put over her ghost stories.
The audience were probably eating them up with spoons.

He glanced around to see how everyone else was reacting.
Diana was bored, and not even trying to hide it. Toby looked
almost defiantly unimpressed, and even Indira looked pretty
sceptical. And Leslie . . . paid June no attention at all, lost in
his own thoughts.

June finished her last story with the expected dramatic
flourish: 'And when he looked round, *there was no one there!*'

Alistair waited a moment, to be sure that was it, and then
applauded politely. The others joined in, probably in the hope
that would be enough to keep June from starting up again.
She took one last look around the kitchen, making sure she
hadn't forgotten anything, and then nodded quickly.

'All right, that's it, job done. Now, let's get the hell out of
here, before we catch something that laughs in the face
of penicillin.'

She gestured sharply for everyone to back away, and the
group filed obediently out of the kitchen. June pulled
the kitchen door shut, and started towards the toilet.

'Trust me, you do not want to go in there,' Toby said quickly.
'Not unless nature is calling in a positively deafening voice.'

'Is it really that bad?' said Indira.

'Worse,' said Toby.

June took in the expressions on her guests' faces, and had
the good sense to recognize a brewing mutiny when she saw
one. She scowled, just a bit petulantly.

'I had some good stories associated with that toilet . . . The
audience would have gone crazy over them.'

'Tell your stories out here,' said Alistair.

June glared at the closed toilet door. 'They wouldn't have
the same impact.'

'Hold everything and stamp on the brake,' said Indira. 'I
only just made the connection . . . You put a camera inside
the toilet?'

'Of course,' said June. 'They're everywhere. We can't risk

missing something important.' She caught the sudden look on Toby's face, and showed him something very like a genuine smile. 'Don't worry; the director can pixelate anything big enough to show up on camera.'

'That does it,' said Diana. 'I am holding it in until this show is over.'

'You could always piss in the kitchen sink,' said Toby. 'I've done that often enough when I'm on tour.'

'Wouldn't surprise me in the least,' said Diana. 'Though I have to admit, I did once pee on a potted plant, in an emergency.'

'That doesn't sound so bad,' said Alistair.

'I was on stage at the time,' said Diana.

June shook her head, and headed back to the main hall.

'What about the storeroom?' said Alistair.

June stopped and looked back at him. 'I don't have any stories set in there. It's just a storeroom.'

Indira frowned. 'But if ghosts walked through the kitchen wall, they should have ended up in that room.'

Diana smiled at her kindly. 'It is possible that you're over-thinking this, dear.'

June looked as if she wanted to say something cutting, but rose above it. She strode back into the main hall, and everyone else followed her in. After leaving the comparatively bright light of the foyer for the deep gloom of the hall, it seemed to Alistair that the shadows were actually deeper and darker than before. He tilted his head back to study the ceiling. Diana moved in beside him.

'Alistair; what are you doing?'

'Counting the lights, to check whether any more of them have gone out in our absence.'

'And?' said Diana.

'The number hasn't changed.'

'Then why does it seem darker now?'

'I'm working on that.'

Toby and Indira overheard what they were saying, and moved closer together. June strode unconcernedly down the hall, kicking her way through the laid-out sleeping bags with fine indifference. Leslie trailed along in her wake. Alistair realized June had a destination in mind, and went after them. The rest of the guests brought up the rear, until June finally came to a halt before the raised stage at the far end of the hall.

'Do you expect us to put on a show, and sing for our supper?' Diana said sweetly. 'Or do we have to suffer through more unlikely tales of ghostly goings-on connected to the stage?'

'There isn't an inch of this hall that hasn't acquired some supernatural baggage,' said June. 'Doors opening and closing on their own. Faces at the windows, peering out. Voices, whispering in people's ears . . .'

'Do ghosts walk through these walls as well?' said Indira.

'All the time,' said June.

'Why can't they just use the door?' said Toby.

'Because if the ghosts are part of the past,' Indira said earnestly, 'the door might not be there, for them. The hall itself might not be there.'

'You're overthinking things again, dear,' said Diana.

'Still!' Toby said brightly. 'At least we haven't heard any more spooky footsteps! Though given that we are standing before a stage, I suppose it's always possible we could pick up some old tap-dancing routines, from past performances.'

'What about ventriloquists?' said Indira. 'Throwing their voices across the years!'

Toby scowled. 'Vent acts are creepy. Their dummies always look like things that have died and then been dug up again.'

Indira had to put both hands over her mouth, to hold back the giggles.

Alistair glanced at Leslie, who was being uncharacteristically quiet, given that they were discussing ghosts. He didn't seem to be paying any attention to the group; just frowning hard, as though listening for something. Alistair moved in beside him.

'Is everything all right, Leslie? Are you picking up on something?'

'Aren't you?' said Leslie.

'Not really, no,' said Alistair.

'There are six of us in the group,' Leslie said carefully.

'Two hosts, and four guests. So why do I keep feeling there are seven of us?'

In spite of himself, Alistair looked quickly around and counted off six people.

'It's like catching glimpses of someone who shouldn't be here, out of the corner of my eye,' said Leslie.

Alistair studied him carefully. 'Are you saying a ghost has joined our little group?'

'It might be a ghost,' said Leslie. 'Or it might be something worse.'

He moved away, to stand beside June. He tried to talk to her, but it was clear she didn't want to hear. Alistair did another quick head count, and still only came up with six. He shrugged, and went back to Diana. June gestured grandly at the stage, and raised her voice.

'Take a good look, people; this stage has been part of the hall since it was first constructed. All kinds of performers have appeared on it, down the years. And once . . . an actor actually died treading these very boards.'

'We've all died on stage at one time or another, darling,' Diana said dryly.

'But I mean really died,' said June. 'Dropped down dead, for no reason, right in the middle of his big speech.'

'Then he's probably still here,' said Diana. 'Waiting for his chance to finish it. Do you happen to know which play it was?'

June looked at her. 'What possible difference could that make?'

Alistair grinned. 'It could have been *Death of a Salesman.*'

Toby groaned loudly.

'Has anyone actually seen this phantom of the hall?' said Alistair.

June smiled widely, embracing the moment. 'Many actors have reported feeling an extra presence on this stage . . . as though there was one more cast member present than the scene called for.'

Alistair shot a quick glance at Leslie, but the medium had nothing to say.

'Come along, people,' said June. 'I have so much more to show you.'

She led them round the stage and pulled back the hanging curtain to reveal a concealed door that opened on to a dark stairway. She fumbled around till she found the light switch, and a single hanging bulb halfway up the stairs glowed as bravely as it could manage, under the circumstances. June led the way up the narrow stairway, and everyone else followed behind in single file. They packed the narrow space so tightly with their bodies that they blocked out most of the light. Alistair really didn't like the way the wooden steps creaked so loudly under their weight, as though warning that someone was coming. And then he thought: *Warning who?*

They finally emerged into a pokey little dressing room, tucked away under arching roof beams. Everyone crowded together at the top of the stairs, as June searched for the light switch. It took her a while to find it, and the group stirred uneasily in the gloom, imagining dim shapes stirring in the deep dark shadows of the dressing room. June finally made a satisfied sound and another lone bulb flared into life, pushing back as many of the shadows as it could. There didn't seem to be much to look at. Just a few dusty tables, some smeared makeup mirrors, and a clothing rail with no clothes.

'Is there anything sadder than a deserted dressing room?' Diana said wistfully. 'They're usually so full of life and laughter, gossip and bitchery.'

'The magic of the theatre,' Alistair said solemnly.

'Got it in one, darling!' said Diana.

'There's something wrong with this place,' Indira said quietly. 'It feels as though there are still people here, hiding in plain sight. I can't tell whether that's because the room is so empty, or because it isn't empty enough.'

Everyone could hear the simple sincerity in her voice. Diana quickly cut in.

'All old dressing rooms feel a bit haunted, dear. So many people pass through them, they can't help but leave a little of themselves behind.'

'That's why they always smell of disinfectant,' said Toby.

Alistair turned to June. 'Are you about to tell us that someone died here, as well?'

'No,' June said cheerfully. 'Something much worse than

that. You'll have noticed how dusty this room is. That's because no one wants to use it any more. Not after what happened.'

'All right,' Alistair said politely. 'I'll play your straight man. What did happen?'

'A group of amateur theatricals were putting on a play in the hall,' said June. 'On one particular evening, no different from any other, they were all up busy getting changed into costumes, or sitting in front of the mirrors to put on their makeup. Chatting away quite happily, by all accounts. Nothing to suggest that anything might be wrong. Then one woman suddenly stopped talking, right in the middle of a sentence. Her friend sitting next to her turned to see what the problem was, and found the woman wasn't there. Her chair was empty.

'The friend looked around the dressing room, but there was no sign of the missing woman anywhere. The friend called out to the other actors, asking if they'd seen the woman leave the room, but no one had. They were all quite adamant the woman couldn't have passed them on the way to the only door without them noticing. They called out to the missing woman, increasingly loudly, but there was no reply. Between one moment and the next, the woman had suddenly and silently disappeared.

'Eventually everyone fell silent, and looked at each other. And that was when they heard the missing woman's voice, calling out to them for help. It was very quiet, coming from somewhere far away, and growing steadily more distant . . . as though the woman was being dragged off against her will. Afterwards, the actors couldn't even agree on which direction the voice had been coming from. It finally faded out, and was gone; and that was the last anyone ever heard of the missing woman.'

For a long moment none of the group said anything, stunned into silence by the brutal simplicity of the tale. They stood very still, listening hard, as though half expecting to hear a distant voice . . .

'OK . . .' Diana said finally. 'That was real theatrical bullshit. And I should know.'

Alistair wasn't so sure. Of all the stories he'd heard so far, this one had the quiet ring of authenticity. Not least because

it wasn't a ghost story. If it had been, the missing woman or
her voice would have turned up again to haunt the hall. And
there was no way June would have left out a juicy detail like
that.

The group peered unhappily round the dressing room. It
didn't take them long to realize there was nowhere the woman
could have gone, without being seen. And not even a trace of
a clue, to help them understand what might have happened.
Just a general feeling that if one person could disappear . . .
maybe someone else could too. The guests started edging back
to the door, and June realized she had to act quickly to prevent
a stampede.

'Let's go back down, people. We still have work to do.'

The quiet, business-like tone of her voice helped settle the
guests, and they filed obediently back through the door and
down the narrow stairs. Alistair was the last to leave, and he
paused at the top of the stairs to watch June hesitate by
the light switch. She looked as though she was trying to decide
whether it was safe to turn off the light. Or whether something
might come out of the dark after her. And Alistair had to
wonder if June had told her story so well she'd spooked herself,
or if this was just another of her performances for the audience. In the end June made a sharp, impatient sound, turned
off the light, and headed for the stairs.

Alistair made sure he was already well on his way down
by the time June caught up with him. She wouldn't have
wanted him to see her moment of weakness. She soon crowded
in behind him, yelling for everyone else to get a move on.
The guests clattered loudly down the stairs and out into the
main hall, and then moved quickly away from the concealed
door, clearly relieved to be back among more familiar shadows.

'Are you sure there aren't any secret doors in this place?'
said Toby. 'Maybe even a few hidden passages? Only that
would explain a lot . . .'

'I thought such things came as standard, in all good haunted
houses,' said Diana. 'Like creaking door hinges, and cobwebs
on the butler.'

'Our technical people spent days tearing this place apart,'
Leslie said patiently, 'so they could install the cameras, and

all the necessary sound systems. If they had found anything like that, they would have said something. And they didn't.'

'Not even a trapdoor in the stage?' said Diana.

'Well, yes,' said June. 'There is one of those. We had to have it sealed off and made secure, to satisfy health and safety.'

'On a ghost show?' said Alistair.

'Oh, you'd be amazed at the song and dance they put us through,' said June, her eyes sparkling with the memory of old battles. 'All the precautions and safety checks before they'd sign off on the show. We even had to agree to take out extra insurance, in case one of you happened to fall and damage yourselves, jumping at some unexpected noise.'

'What about life insurance?' said Toby. 'In case one of us gets frightened to death?'

'We did ask,' said Leslie. 'It would have made for great publicity. But no one would cover us. Apparently ghosts fall under "Acts of God".'

Everyone turned to look at Alistair, who spread his hands apologetically.

'Mysterious ways, my friends.'

'I never believed in life insurance,' Diana said loudly. 'That just means someone else has a vested interest in you being dead.'

'Understandable, in your case,' said Toby.

'So!' Indira said quickly. 'What are we supposed to do now?'

June made a point of checking her watch. 'We need to pace ourselves, or we'll all start wilting long before the end of the show. I've told some good stories, and you provided some useful reactions, so I think we've thrown enough raw meat to the animals for now. Our director will need time to sort out some appropriate documentaries, to put it all in context, so we might as well get a little rest. Take an hour off, and sack out in the sleeping bags. That's what they're for.'

'Are you kidding?' said Diana. 'I have never felt less like sleeping in my entire life.'

There was a general murmur of agreement from the guests, along with much nodding of heads.

'That's just the tension and adrenalin speaking,' said Leslie.

'Trust me, once you're off your feet and lying down, you'll
be amazed at how fast it all catches up with you. So take a
break and recharge your batteries, because you're going to
need everything you've got to make it all the way to
the finishing line.'

The guests looked at each other, smiled or shrugged as the
mood took them, and then arranged themselves as best they
could on their sleeping bags. Alistair sat with his arms wrapped
around his knees, pulled up tight to his chest. He wasn't sure
he understood what was going on. He hadn't seen one of these
shows before, but it did seem odd to him that although they'd
been on air for some time, they hadn't actually done much.
Of course, June and Leslie had run so many of these shows
they should know what they were doing . . .

Alistair pushed the thought away, for the moment, and
looked around the group. He did another quick head count, to
confirm there were only six of them, with not even a sniff of
a seventh; and then he smiled and shrugged, quietly annoyed
that he'd allowed Leslie to get to him. He kept a watchful eye
on the group as one by one they made themselves as comfortable as possible on their sleeping bags. June and Leslie
stretched out side by side with practised nonchalance, apparently not in the least bothered at the prospect of nodding off
in the company of strangers. Presumably because they'd done
it so many times before.

Alistair was interested to note that no one had opened their
sleeping bags and climbed inside. Instead, they'd all chosen
to rest on top of them. Presumably because each of them had
been troubled by the same idea; that if something bad did turn
up, they didn't want to be caught zipped inside their bags and
helpless. Toby and Indira sat close together on adjoining
sleeping bags, talking quietly. Alistair just happened to lean
in their direction, so he could eavesdrop on what they were
saying.

'I'll never get to sleep,' said Indira. She sat huddled, drawn
in on herself, shooting anxious glances round the hall.

'You're perfectly safe,' said Toby. 'I'm here.'

'It's the shadows,' said Indira. 'So dark, anything could be
hiding inside them.'

She sounded as though the evening's stress had driven her back to the fears of her childhood, when a monster could be lurking anywhere she couldn't see.

'I won't let anything happen to you,' said Toby. 'If there are any ghosts in this dump, they'll have to get past me to get to you; and that's not going to happen.'

Indira smiled at him. 'What did I do, to deserve a protector like you?'

Toby grinned. 'Just lucky, I guess.'

They laughed softly together, and when Toby finally settled back on his sleeping bag, Indira did too. They lay on their sides, so they could face each other. Indira looked trustingly at Toby, who looked quietly pleased at being trusted. And determined to be worthy of it.

Alistair turned away to look at Diana, who was lying stiffly on her back on the sleeping bag next to his. Her arms were tightly folded, and she stared defiantly up at the ceiling, as though determined not to close her eyes for a moment. Alistair lay back on his sleeping bag, and arranged his long limbs as comfortably as possible. Diana suddenly turned her head to look at him, and when she spoke she pitched her voice low enough that only he would hear her.

'Tell me, Bish . . . Just how convinced are you, by everything that's happened so far?'

'Not much,' said Alistair, just as quietly. 'The lights going out could have been arranged in advance, to establish the right look for this kind of show. And to put the wind up the guests, of course. And I do find it very suspicious that all our phones just happened to stop working. I'd put my money on some kind of jammer. Remember the state-of-the-art ghost-hunting tech they boasted about? As for the sounds we thought were footsteps . . . Well, you already know what I think about them.'

'What about Leslie, and his trance?' Diana said carefully.

She was trying hard to keep her voice light and casual, but Alistair could hear how much effort went into that. He kept his own voice carefully calm.

'I think he was so desperate to put on a good show, he ended up hypnotizing himself.'

'And the things he said?'

'Educated guesses, based on the homework he did before he came here.'

Diana nodded slowly. 'Yes, that makes sense. You're probably right.'

'I'm always right,' said Alistair. 'It comes with the job.'

Diana met his gaze for a long moment. 'You make me feel very safe and secure, Alistair. Is that part of your job too?'

'Not necessarily,' said Alistair.

They looked into each other's eyes, and smiled the same kind of smile.

'I did tell you not to trust June or Leslie,' said Diana.

'So you did,' said Alistair. 'They've been manipulating all of us, ever since they arrived.'

Diana frowned. 'But what about the cold spot?'

'What about it?' Alistair said politely.

'That was real, wasn't it?'

'I didn't feel any drop in temperature,' said Alistair. 'Did you?'

Diana thought about it. 'I'm not sure. I thought I did . . .'

'June and Leslie said it was cold, and then they both shuddered convincingly. But their breath didn't steam on the air. Which is what you would have expected, if the temperature really had plummeted.'

Diana grinned, genuinely delighted. 'Well spotted, Bish! I knew they'd be putting on a performance for the people at home, but now I'm starting to wonder just how far they would go, to convince us something genuinely was happening here.'

'It's not just about us,' said Alistair.

Diana smiled dazzlingly. 'Darling, as long as I'm on camera, it's always going to be all about me.' She stretched languorously, and settled herself more comfortably on her sleeping bag. 'You know, Leslie was right about one thing. I do feel tired.'

'Get some sleep,' said Alistair. 'I'll keep watch, for a while.'

'Aren't you tired?' said Diana. Her eyes were closed, and already her voice was blurred by approaching sleep.

'If I have to, I'll sleep with one ear open,' said Alistair. 'Nothing's going to creep up on us.'

A slow heavy silence fell across the hall, as one by one everyone fell asleep. And that included Alistair, who found he couldn't keep his eyes open, no matter how hard he tried. And then he was suddenly wide awake again, as June's wristwatch alarm went off. He raised himself on one elbow and looked blearily around him, as June sat up and turned the alarm off.

'Everybody up!' she said loudly. 'You've had your nice nap, but now it's back to work!'

She scrambled up on to her feet, put one hand to her beehive hairdo to make sure it had survived intact, and then moved around the circle of sleeping bags, calling out names and giving shoulders a good shake. Leslie came to with a jolt and sat quickly up to peer around the hall, as though checking whether anything had changed while he was asleep. Alistair stretched slowly, trying to ease his back muscles, which were really not happy about sleeping on a wooden floor with only a sleeping bag to provide a cushion. Diana sat up beside him, looking prettily tousled, and then bent over and coughed harshly.

'God, I'd kill for a cigarette,' she said. 'My agent insisted I give them up, because so many people won't work with smokers.'

'Good for him,' said Alistair.

'Puritan,' said Diana. She shot him a sideways glance. 'I've never slept beside a bishop before.'

'You should get out more,' Alistair said solemnly.

Diana chuckled earthily. 'Oh I have, darling. Want to hear my confessions?'

'If you'll hear mine,' said Alistair.

June had to shake Toby's shoulder hard, and shout right into his ear, before he finally lurched upright and shook her off. He then cursed her, and the world in general, as he massaged his aching forehead with both hands. June left him to it, and moved on. She called out Indira's name, and bent right over to give her shoulder a good shake, but Indira still didn't respond. By then the whole group was looking round to see what was happening. Toby suddenly surged forward and pushed June out of the way so he could kneel beside

Indira, who was lying on her side with her back to him. He turned her over, and that was when everyone saw that Indira's eyes were wide open and staring sightlessly. Fixed on something only the dead could see.

FIVE
After She Died

E ven with a dead woman at his feet, and chaos breaking out all around him, Alistair couldn't keep from studying everyone else's reactions. At first everyone just seemed lost and confused, pressing in for a closer look and babbling loudly, unable to believe Indira was really dead. But they all stopped and fell silent when Toby picked up Indira's body and cradled it in his arms.

His shoulders shook and his face convulsed, but he didn't cry. Diana started forward, but Alistair stopped her with a hand on her arm. He could see anger as well as grief in Toby's face. Alistair glanced quickly at June and Leslie, but they were both standing well back, unsure as to what they should do. Toby finally looked up from Indira, and there was nothing left in his face but pain.

'She was going to be the daughter I always wanted, and never had,' he said. 'I'd only just found her . . . and now she's been taken away. It's not fair.'

Alistair moved cautiously forward, and knelt down beside Toby. 'No, it isn't. But right now I need you to set Indira down, Toby, so I can examine her.'

'She's dead!' said Toby.

'Yes,' said Alistair. 'I think she is. But we have to be sure.'

For a moment Alistair thought Toby might defy him, but then Toby sighed tiredly and gently lowered Indira back on to her sleeping bag. He patted her shoulder once, like a father comforting a sleeping child, and then stood up and stepped back to give Alistair room to work. Diana put a comforting arm across Toby's shoulders, but he didn't even seem to know she was there. Diana hugged him anyway.

Alistair checked Indira's wrist and throat for a pulse, pressed his ear against her chest so he could listen for a heartbeat, and finally took off his glasses and held them close to Indira's mouth; but there wasn't even a trace of breath to fog the lenses. Alistair sighed quietly, put his glasses back on, and got to his feet. Toby looked numbly at Alistair, silently pleading for an answer he knew he wasn't going to get.

'I'm sorry, Toby,' said Alistair. 'There's nothing I can do. She's gone.'

Toby tried to say something, but the words wouldn't come. He turned and walked away, his shoulders hitching as he struggled to get his breath. Diana looked unhappily after him, but let him go. June took a step forward, looked at Indira's body, and then turned to Alistair. Her professional air was gone, torn away. She looked shocked, thrown off balance by something that should never have happened. She had to struggle to keep her voice steady.

'How did she die?'

'I can't tell,' said Alistair. 'There are no obvious injuries.'

'She couldn't just have died in her sleep,' said Diana. 'Not a healthy young woman like that.'

'But if there's no injuries, it must have been natural causes,' said June. And just like that, the professional persona was back in place. She sounded as though she was rehearsing a statement for the press. 'Perhaps the stressful nature of the show was too much for her.'

Toby spun back to face her, his voice so full of anger it didn't even sound like him.

'She wasn't that scared! And anyway, she knew she had me to look after her!'

'Could it be something to do with the hall?' said Diana, trying hard to sound diplomatic. 'I'm thinking of the actor who dropped dead on stage, and no one knew why.'

'And more recently, there was Albert Matheson,' said Alistair. 'Two previous unexplained deaths in the same location has to mean something . . .'

And then he stopped, as he caught a glimpse of something in June's face. He closed in on her, holding her gaze with his.

'You know something,' he said, not even trying to hide the accusation in his voice. 'Have there been other unexplained deaths in this hall?'

June tore her gaze away from his, and looked to Leslie for support; but he was still staring at the dead woman. Left on her own, June had no choice but to turn back to Alistair. 'You can't expect me to know everything,' she said defensively.

Any other time, Alistair would have laughed in her face. 'You wouldn't have chosen this setting for your show unless you'd done a hell of a lot of research. Making sure you knew everything there was to know, if only so you could use it to your advantage. How many mysterious deaths have there been in this place?'

'Tell him,' said Leslie, not looking round.

June nodded, reluctantly. 'All together, down the years . . . Twenty-seven.'

Diana gasped, and looked quickly at the surrounding shadows. Leslie hung his head and hunched his shoulders. Toby looked disbelievingly at June, and then he stalked towards her, his hands closed into fists.

'How could you not tell us something like that?'

June tried to back away from Toby, only to find Diana had moved in behind her, blocking the way.

'This isn't a haunted hall!' Diana said angrily. 'It's a slaughterhouse!'

'You see!' said June, her voice rising as she glared around her. 'That reaction, right there, is why I didn't tell anyone! Because I knew you'd overreact. It's just a statistical anomaly! It doesn't mean anything.'

Diana grabbed June by the shoulder and spun her round, so she could glare right into her face.

'Twenty-seven deaths doesn't mean anything? How can you say that?'

'Because we did the research!' June said loudly, throwing off Diana's hand.

'There was a full official investigation into every death,' said Leslie. He'd finally raised his head, and his face was calm and composed. 'There was even a separate inquiry into the hall itself, in case there might be hidden environmental factors. But none of them uncovered any evidence of anything unusual.'

'We acquired copies of all the reports, and worked our way

through them,' said June. 'There was nothing there! Not a fact, not a conjecture; nothing to even suggest why so many people might have died. Come on, think it through! Do you honestly believe Leslie and I would be here, if we thought we were in any danger?'

'So who killed Indira?' said Toby. 'The ghosties and ghoulies?'

'It is possible,' said Leslie.

Everyone turned to look at him.

'I've been thinking,' Leslie said quietly. 'What if Indira woke up, and saw something that disturbed her so greatly her heart just gave out?'

No one said anything. Alistair could see that none of them wanted to accept this new idea, but despite themselves, it was taking hold. One by one they turned away to look around the hall, and the shadows stared back at them, deep and dark, holding secrets within. Everyone moved closer together, like animals at a watering hole who'd caught the scent of a predator.

'Could there be something in the hall, after all?' said Diana. 'Something old and terrible that wants us all dead?'

'Do you have to be so theatrical?' said June.

'Why would ghosts want to kill anyone?' said Toby.

'Ghosts used to be people,' said Leslie. 'Which means they can be good, or bad. If something in this place felt threatened by our presence . . .'

'But why kill Indira?' Toby said plaintively. 'She never did anything to hurt anyone.'

Leslie shrugged. 'The ghosts had to start somewhere . . .'

Diana looked at him sharply. 'You think there might be more than one thing threatening us?'

'The hall has been here a long time,' said Leslie. 'Long enough to absorb the pain and horror of a great many lives . . .'

'There's nothing dangerous here!' said June. Alistair thought she sounded mostly irritated, as though the main problem with Indira's death was that it was interrupting her show. June looked quickly from face to face, and made a clear effort to sound calm and reasonable. 'We never expected anything like this to happen. We've never had any trouble on this show before. It's just entertainment!'

'I'll bet an awful lot of people are watching the show now,' Alistair said thoughtfully. 'All of them waiting eagerly to see what will happen next.'

'You mean, waiting to see if someone else will die?' said Diana. 'Oh, that's just ghoulish.'

'That's entertainment,' said Leslie.

June turned on him. 'Will you shut up!'

He didn't even look at her. June turned away to find Toby had moved in close, so he could stare right into her face.

'You should have warned us. Made it clear what we were getting into. You let us walk into a trap!'

'I didn't know,' June said stubbornly. 'How could I? And anyway, you all signed waivers, indemnifying this show against any claims—'

'Twenty-seven deaths!' Diana said loudly. 'How could you not know?'

'There are always stories, wherever you go,' said June.

'Twenty-seven confirmed deaths is more than just a story,' said Alistair. 'I can't believe I haven't heard about this before.'

'No one put the pieces together,' said June. 'Possibly because they didn't want to. After all, if the tourists got to hear about it . . .'

She broke off, as Toby thrust his face right into hers. When he spoke, his voice was very cold and very dangerous.

'I will spend the rest of my life making sure you get everything that's coming to you.'

'Give it your best shot,' said June. 'Better than you have tried.' She took a deep breath, and made herself adopt a more reasonable tone. 'I never believed in any of the scary stuff before tonight, any more than you did. And now I'm in as much danger as the rest of you.'

'Do you believe someone else is going to die?' said Alistair.

'Don't you?' said June.

'There's no evidence that Indira's death was caused by things not of this world,' Alistair said carefully. 'It seems far more likely to me that she was murdered.'

That last word seemed to hang on the air, heavy with

significance. Everyone stared at Alistair, and he stared calmly back. Toby frowned, trying to get his head around the idea.

'How could it be murder? She was right here with us. If anything suspicious had happened, we would have noticed.'

'Would we?' said Alistair. 'We were all fast asleep, exhausted by our reactions to the hall. If someone was very quiet, and very determined . . .'

'But there are cameras all around us!' said Diana. 'Who'd be stupid enough to murder someone in front of a whole bunch of live cameras, and God knows how many witnesses?'

'No one human,' said Leslie.

They all turned to look at him.

'I think we woke something up when we installed our equipment,' the medium said steadily. 'Something that doesn't want us here.'

'There's no one in the hall but us!' said June. 'Indira's death was just one of those things!'

Toby slapped June across the face. The force of the blow sent her staggering backwards. Toby started to go after her, but Alistair moved quickly in and grabbed Toby from behind, pinioning his arms to his sides. Toby fought to pull free, but couldn't break Alistair's grip. He stopped struggling and looked at June with lost, empty eyes.

'Indira is dead because of you,' Toby said quietly. 'Why are you still alive, when she's gone?'

June stared back at him, wide-eyed with shock, one hand pressed to her cheek. She didn't say anything.

Alistair spoke quietly into Toby's ear. 'Indira wouldn't want this.'

'Indira doesn't want anything,' said Toby. 'She's dead.'

All the strength seemed to go out of him. Alistair let go, and stepped back to give him some room. Toby turned to face him, and then collapsed into Alistair's arms and pressed his face against his chest, sobbing hard, racking tears that he couldn't hold back any longer. Alistair held Toby close, and patted his shoulder.

'I told her she'd be safe with me,' said Toby. He had to force the words out. 'I promised I'd protect her. I was sleeping right next to her . . . But I never heard a thing.'

'None of us did,' said Alistair.

'Why couldn't it have been me?' said Toby.

Alistair didn't have an answer to that, so he just patted Toby on the shoulder some more. Everyone else just looked at Alistair and Toby, not knowing what to do. After a while Toby straightened up, and stopped crying. Alistair let him go, and realized the tears had stopped not because Toby had run out, but because he'd made up his mind to do something.

'Right,' said Toby. 'That's it. The show is over. We are leaving, and I am calling the police. Let them sort out what happened here.'

He headed for the main doors. June yelled after him.

'You can't leave!'

Toby didn't even glance back at her. 'Try and stop me.'

'You don't understand,' said Leslie. 'The time-locks won't open until tomorrow morning, no matter what.'

Toby slowed to a halt, still facing the exit. 'Then I'll just have to break the doors down.'

'You can't,' said Leslie, his voice full of a terrible patience. 'We had the doors and the locks specially strengthened and reinforced, to make sure no one could get out. In case someone panicked during the show and tried to make a run for it.'

Diana stared at him. 'You were going to keep us trapped in here, against our will?'

'Why would you do something like that?' said Alistair.

'For the drama,' said Leslie. 'That was how we sold this show, in the advance publicity. *Two hosts and four guests, trapped in a situation they can't escape, facing all the powers of darkness!* We knew our audience would go for that, big time.'

'So we're stuck in here with a body?' said Diana. 'And possibly a murderer?'

Toby turned around, and came back to join the group. His sense of purpose wasn't gone, he was just looking for a new outlet for his anger. Everyone looked at everyone else, their faces full of unease and suspicion. Alistair reluctantly decided it was down to him to do something constructive. Because no one else was going to.

'We can't leave Indira lying here,' he said. 'It's not respectful.'

We need to put her somewhere safe and secure, out of harm's way.'

'Why?' said Toby. 'What else can happen to her? She's dead.'

'It's important we preserve whatever evidence might still be present on her person,' said Alistair. 'We don't have to worry about the crime scene, because that's her sleeping bag, and we can move that with her.'

Really, he wanted Indira moved because no one in the group would be able to think clearly as long as the body was still in the room. Once Indira was safely out of sight, they should be able to discuss things more rationally. And there were a lot of things Alistair wanted to talk about.

'Hold it,' Diana said suddenly. 'Wouldn't the cameras have recorded the murder?'

New hope appeared in everyone's face, only to fade away as June shook her head.

'Unfortunately, no. The director turned the cameras off while we were sleeping.'

'Why would he do that?' said Toby.

'Because I told him to!' said June. 'A whole hour of watching us sleep would have bored the arse off our audience.'

'We are in the chills and thrills business,' said Leslie. 'So we had the director run some old ghost documentaries to hold the audience's attention, until we were up and about again.'

Did someone know that? thought Alistair. *And take advantage?* He realized everyone was looking to him, so he pushed the thought to one side, for later.

'Let's move Indira,' he said. 'Grant her some peace, and privacy.'

'Where can we put her?' said Diana.

'The kitchen,' said Alistair. 'It's where she'd feel most at home.'

'Yes,' said Toby. 'She'd like that.'

'But it's so messy in there!' said Diana.

'She won't care,' said Toby.

Alistair organized everyone into picking up the edges of the sleeping bag, so they wouldn't have to touch the body, and then they carefully transported Indira over to the side door, and into the kitchen. They'd just started to put her on the floor when Diana made a sudden unhappy sound.

'What is it?' said Toby.

'The cockroaches are back,' said Diana.

She didn't have to raise the prospect of bugs scuttling over Indira's body if they left her on the floor, because it was already on everyone's mind. So they lifted up the body and placed it carefully across the tops of the ovens. There was just enough room to fit her in. Toby painstakingly tucked the sleeping bag around Indira's body, as though protecting her from the cold.

'Sleep well,' he said quietly.

And then he left the kitchen, followed quickly by June and Leslie. Diana started to go after them, and then stopped and looked at Alistair, when she realized he hadn't moved. Diana glanced out the kitchen door to make sure the others were gone, and then frowned at Alistair.

'Do you honestly think Indira was murdered?'

Alistair nodded. 'That makes a lot more sense to me, than that something supernaturally nasty stuck its face into hers. And she was far too young to have suffered a heart attack, or a seizure.'

'But how can she have been murdered, when there aren't any wounds?'

'Clearly someone put a lot of thought into this murder.'

Diana looked at him. 'You seem to know a lot about preserving evidence, and you weren't at all bothered when it came to examining the corpse. How does a bishop end up knowing about things like that?'

'A lot of young men die before their time in All Souls Hollow,' said Alistair. 'I've seen so many bodies and victims of crime that they don't disturb me any more. And I believe I have a responsibility to work out what happened here . . . So I can keep everyone else safe.'

'You think the killer isn't done with us yet?'

'Either the murderer is hiding somewhere in the hall,' said Alistair. 'Or they must be one of us.'

Diana nodded slowly. 'I'm not sure the others have caught on to that yet.'

'They will,' said Alistair. 'And now, I'm going to say a prayer for the dead. You're welcome to join me, if you wish.'

Diana shook her head. 'I don't go in for that sort of thing. It's not like she can hear us.'

'The point of prayers is to comfort the living,' said Alistair.

Diana took one last look at Indira's body. 'There is no comfort.'

She left the kitchen, her back unyieldingly straight. Alistair quietly closed the door behind her, and then went back to the sleeping bag and carefully pulled the sides away, so he could give Indira's body a proper examination. He took his time, checking her out from head to toe, and still couldn't find anything. No wounds, no bruises, nothing to suggest she'd even tried to defend herself. Whatever happened must have taken place while Indira was still asleep.

Which meant she wouldn't have known anything about it. That was something.

Alistair checked Indira's clothes carefully, and finally discovered a single small drop of blood. It was on the front of her sari, right over the heart. Too small to come from a knife wound; he'd seen enough of those in his time. And too big to be the result of an injection. So what did that leave?

Alistair wondered whether he should undress the body, to see if there was any kind of mark on the skin; but if one of the others should happen to come back in to see what was keeping him, and found him undressing a corpse . . . He stared at the body for a while, thinking hard, and then he closed the sleeping bag around Indira again, and said the prayer for the dead.

When he went back into the hall, June and Leslie were standing together in the midst of the crumpled sleeping bags, their heads close together. Diana and Toby were both standing alone, deep in their own thoughts. All of them looked round quickly as Alistair reappeared, hoping he'd have something new to say that would make them feel better.

'We need to search the hall,' he said firmly. 'If there is a killer, he could be hiding somewhere . . . just waiting for a chance to reappear and kill again.'

The others looked distinctly unhappy. It wasn't what they'd wanted to hear.

'No one could have got past the time-locks,' June said stubbornly. 'We're completely cut off from the world.'

'The only other possibility is that the killer is one of us,' said Alistair.

He could tell from the looks on their faces that they liked that idea even less.

'What possible motive could any of us have, to be a murderer?' said June. 'None of us had even met Indira before today.'

'Which is why a hidden killer seems the most likely explanation,' said Alistair. 'But the only way to be sure is to search the hall from top to bottom.'

'I'm not buying this,' said Toby. 'How could anyone have got in without us knowing?'

'Someone could have entered the hall before we did,' said Alistair. 'Remember all those technicians June hired, to set things up for the show? With so many people coming and going, would anyone notice one more? The murderer could have just slipped away when no one was looking, and then concealed themselves in some unknown hiding place.'

'But how would they know about this unknown hiding place?' said Diana.

'They could have had access to the original architectural plans,' said Alistair.

'OK . . . You're reaching now,' said Diana.

'I know,' said Alistair. 'But do you have a better idea as to what we should be doing?'

'Yes,' said Diana. 'Unfortunately, it involves us not having come here in the first place.'

'We've already been round the hall, and seen everything there is to see,' said June.

'But this time,' said Alistair, 'we're going to make a thorough search.'

Toby's face took on a new determination. 'If we're going after a killer, we're going to need weapons.'

'Well, I'm sorry,' said Diana. 'But I didn't think to bring any sharp and pointed things with me.'

'There could be knives in the kitchen,' said Toby.

Everyone apart from Alistair nodded. They liked the idea of weapons.

'Having a knife would make me feel more secure,' said June.

'Maybe you'll get lucky, and find a back to stick it into,' said Leslie.

June looked at him. 'One more word from you, and I will cut off your residuals.'

Alistair really didn't like the idea of so many nervous people waving sharp-edged weapons around, but he kept the thought to himself, because the others clearly didn't want to hear it. Toby strode over to the side door. Alistair went after him, and everyone else fell in behind. Toby and Alistair entered the kitchen, while the others stayed at the doorway.

'You search the drawers,' Alistair said to Toby. 'I'll check the cupboards.'

It didn't take them long to discover that the drawers and the cupboards were empty of anything even remotely resembling a weapon. Toby stood in the middle of the kitchen and glared about him.

'How can there not be any knives?'

'Someone sold them all off,' said Alistair. 'Going by the state of this kitchen, it's been a long time since anyone did any cooking in here.'

'But then how are we supposed to defend ourselves?' said Toby.

'With our wits,' said Alistair. 'And we do have the advantage of numbers.'

'Unless the killer is one of us,' said Toby.

'You think that's likely?' said Alistair.

'Don't you?'

And then, because he couldn't put it off any longer, Toby turned to face Indira, still cocooned in her sleeping bag.

'She looks like she's at peace,' he said.

'Yes,' said Alistair. 'She does.'

'Do you have any idea who might have done this?'

'No,' said Alistair. 'Do you?'

'Nothing makes sense to me any more,' said Toby.

He started to reach out to the sleeping bag, and then pulled his hand back. He turned to face Alistair.

'What do we do now?'

'We search the storeroom, and the toilet,' said Alistair.

'Really?' said Toby.

'If nothing else, it should help to put everyone's mind at rest,' said Alistair.

Toby shrugged, and led the way out of the kitchen. He didn't look back.

Alistair went straight to the storeroom, and pushed the door all the way open so everyone could see inside. With the sleeping bags and chairs removed, it was just an empty room. Alistair shut the door, looked at the toilet, and then nodded to Toby.

'You know it better than the rest of us.'

'I always get the shit jobs,' said Toby.

He pushed the toilet door open, and everyone recoiled and made some kind of shocked noise, as the smell got out.

'What did you do in there, Toby?' said Diana, waving a hand defensively in front of her face.

'Don't blame it on me!' he said. 'This is how I found it.' He gestured around the empty toilet, and then looked severely at Alistair. 'No one could bear to hide in there for any length of time. Are you satisfied now?'

'It's one less room to worry about,' said Alistair.

Toby pulled the door shut. The toilet's distinctive aroma still lingered on the air, like an unwanted guest who just wouldn't leave. Diana glowered at June.

'All those technicians, and you couldn't spare someone to clean out the toilet and the kitchen?'

'We were pushing the edge of the budget,' Leslie said apologetically. 'We had to save money where we could.'

And that was when the toilet flushed itself. The rushing water sounded very loud on the quiet. Everyone stared at the closed toilet door.

'OK,' said Diana. 'That was just a bit spooky. How could that happen? There was no one in there.'

Alistair looked at Leslie. 'Do ghosts need a toilet?'

'Funny you should say that,' said Leslie. 'Some people claim that ectoplasm . . .'

'Even more don't,' June said crushingly.

'It's just a malfunction,' said Toby. 'I warned you not to trust that flush.'

Back in the main hall, everyone looked expectantly at Alistair. Accepting him as leader because he was the only one with any ideas on what to do. He thought for a moment, and then pointed to the raised stage at the far end of the hall.

'We need to check the upstairs dressing room. We didn't spend long there, so we might have missed something.'

June nodded, and led the way to the concealed door beside the stage. She pushed it open and turned on the light, and then everyone huddled together at the foot of the narrow stairs, remembering how dark the way up had seemed. None of them wanted to go back into that gloom, now there might be a killer lurking. Diana scowled at June.

'I can't believe you didn't think to bring a torch with you.'

'Actually . . .' said Leslie.

'All right!' said June. 'I was just about to tell them!' She looked around her, scowling defensively. 'I do have a torch.'

'You mean we've been stumbling around in the dark all this time when we didn't need to?' said Toby, his voice rising just a bit dangerously.

'Why didn't you use the torch before?' said Diana.

'Because the shadows and the gloom were all part of the drama!' said June. 'I kept the torch handy, in case of an emergency.'

'I'd say this qualifies,' said Alistair.

June produced a long torch from inside the top of one boot, and flashed a beam of light up the narrow stairway. Somewhat emboldened, the group followed June up the creaking stairs and into the long dressing room tucked away under the rafters. The single light bulb revealed the same completely empty space, but this time Alistair made the others wait by the doorway while he checked the walls for hidden doors and sliding panels. He didn't find any, but then he never really thought he would. He was just making a point to the rest of the group: that the hidden murderer was only a theory, which he was painstakingly disproving. Because until they were convinced of that, they'd never be able to accept that the murderer had to be one of them.

And besides, he'd feel such an idiot if he didn't check, and there was someone tucked away in the hall's equivalent of a priest hole. It was about as likely as Casper the Homicidal Ghost, but Alistair didn't feel like taking any chances.

When he was finally done, he nodded to the group at the doorway.

'All done, all clear. One less place to worry about.'

'If you've quite finished tapping on walls and hoping no one will knock back, can we please go back down again?' said Diana. 'Before we all fade away like that unfortunate woman, and leave nothing behind but our reputations?'

'Of course,' said Alistair. 'We still have the main hall to search.'

Once they were safely down the stairs again, Alistair fixed everyone with his best decisive stare. He needed to keep them moving, because his assumed authority wouldn't last much longer.

'Look for anything out of the ordinary,' he said. 'I know the technicians said they'd given this whole area the once-over, but I'm in no mood to trust anyone at the moment. So, we take our time and we don't stop until there's nowhere left to check.'

'Stick close together,' Leslie said quietly. 'We don't want to get picked off one by one.'

'Are you thinking about murderers, or ghosts?' said Diana.

'They're both dangerous,' said Leslie.

They all looked at him, and then at each other. Alistair quickly got them moving again, and they set off round the hall. They checked the walls, foot by foot, tapping carefully and listening for hollow sounds, but didn't find anything. When they reached the main doors, Alistair grabbed hold of the handles with both hands, and rattled them as hard as he could, just in case; but the doors didn't budge. The group made a full circle of the hall and ended up back before the raised stage, and then they all took it in turns to look mutinously at Alistair. Because they were all really tired, and didn't care who knew it. Diana suddenly raised her head, and gestured at the stage.

'What about the trapdoor?'

'What about it?' said June, just a bit snappishly. 'Health and safety made us seal it shut, remember?'

'But you didn't do it yourself,' Alistair said thoughtfully.

'Of course not,' said Leslie. 'She has people to do that kind of thing for her. Heaven forfend she should actually have to work for a living.'

'I work harder than you when I'm asleep,' said June.

'The point is,' said Alistair, 'you don't know for certain that the work was actually done.'

Everyone stared at him resentfully, but he just stared back at them until they gave in and climbed up on to the stage. Tired as they were, they still needed to be sure. The trapdoor turned out to be right in the middle of the stage, looking very obvious and very ordinary.

'I was expecting it to be nailed shut,' said Diana.

'Maybe it is, from underneath,' said Toby.

Diana looked at him pityingly. 'If someone nailed the trapdoor shut from underneath; how would they get out?'

'There must be a way,' Toby said reasonably. 'Or why have a trapdoor in the first place?'

Diana nodded, and looked to June. 'Is there a way out, under the stage?'

'There's a door,' said June. 'But that was nailed shut. I watched them do it. And health and safety made us use superglue all along the trapdoor's edges. Nothing could move it now.'

Toby stamped hard on the trapdoor, several times. The wood didn't even quiver.

They left the stage, and headed back to the circle of sleeping bags, without even glancing at Alistair for permission. Because they all really needed to sit down. They dropped on to their respective chairs with loud groans, and stretched out their legs. Alistair joined them, without saying anything.

'So,' Toby said finally. 'Now we have eliminated all the other possibilities . . . It's clear the killer must be one of us.'

'You're dismissing the possibility that something super-natural could be involved?' Leslie said mildly.

'Yes!' Diana said loudly. 'And none of us want to hear any more of that nonsense!'

'Because it scares you?' said Leslie.

Diana met his gaze coldly. 'Only people can be really scary.'

'One of us must have pretended to go to sleep,' Toby said doggedly. 'They waited until they were sure everyone else had nodded off, and then moved silently round the circle . . . and murdered Indira.'

'How?' said Alistair.

There was a long pause. That single implacable word hung on the air, given weight by its lack of any obvious answer.

'And when they were done,' Toby said finally, 'they just lay down again and waited for someone to discover the body.'

Diana stirred uncomfortably on her chair. 'They'd have to be really cold-blooded . . .'

'Given that the method must have been worked out well in advance,' said Alistair, 'cold-blooded sounds perfectly right.'

'But why would anyone put so much thought and effort into murdering a really minor celebrity like Indira?' said June.

'Someone who'd tried one of her recipes,' said Leslie.

Diana glared at him. 'Really not the right moment.'

'None of this makes any sense,' said June.

'It will,' said Alistair. 'Once we have all the facts.'

'Why didn't we leave someone on guard?' said Toby.

'Who would have thought we needed someone to watch over us while we slept?' said June. 'We've done it before, on other shows, and nothing ever went wrong.'

'Why did you start doing that?' said Alistair.

'Because things went on too long,' Leslie said bluntly. 'And people started falling asleep – on the show, and at home.'

'Who knew there was anything to guard against?' June said forcefully.

She looked accusingly at everyone in turn, and for once Alistair had nothing to say. Diana looked at him steadily.

'You told me you were going to sit up on guard.'

'I meant to,' said Alistair.

'So what happened?' said June.

'I was as tired as everyone else,' said Alistair. 'I just couldn't keep my eyes open.'

Diana nodded. 'And now you feel like you failed to protect Indira. That's why you've been putting yourself in charge, and pushing us to get things done.'

'Yes,' said Alistair. 'As penance.'

'It wasn't your fault,' said Toby.

Alistair nodded his thanks, for that kindness. But he didn't believe it.

They all sat in silence for a while, thinking their own thoughts. Eventually Toby leaned forward on his chair, frowning hard.

'If one of us is the killer, there has to be a motive.'

'But none of us knew Indira,' June said stubbornly. 'We were all strangers to each other, before we turned up here. All right, except for Leslie and me. I've known him for years. And while, God knows, I have more than enough reasons to want to kill him, I never would. I need him for the show.'

'That's the nicest thing you've ever said to me,' said Leslie.

June shot him a brief smile. 'Make the most of it.'

Alistair studied the two hosts thoughtfully. 'We still haven't established why you chose us, specifically, as guests? Especially such a minor celebrity as Indira.'

'June did all the choosing,' Leslie said immediately. 'I wasn't even consulted. I never am.'

June stared at him. 'You can turn on me like that, after I just defended you?'

'Is that what that was?' said Leslie.

June looked round the circle, glowering from one face to the next. 'What was I supposed to do? Send you all a questionnaire, with a note saying *Please tick this box to show you're not a robot or a murderer*?'

'But why choose us?' said Alistair, raising his voice a little to make it clear he wasn't going to stop asking the question until he got an answer.

'None of you were my first choice,' said June. 'I actually

had a much better class of guests in mind; but they either weren't available, or we couldn't afford them.'

Toby was so intrigued he allowed himself to be sidetracked. 'Who did you really want?'

June stared coldly back at him. 'My first choice for comic relief was Tommy Buttons.'

Toby sat bolt upright, so outraged he forgot how tired he was. 'What does he have that I don't?'

'A career,' said June. She turned abruptly to stare at Alistair. 'For the God-bothering slot, I had my heart set on that charismatic new television evangelist, Saint Jack Saint; but he said he wouldn't lower himself to appear on a show like this.'

'Good for him,' said Alistair.

June turned to Diana. 'We came really close to getting Dame Lucy Tremaire, the national treasure; but she kept adding so many extras to her rider that we were forced to give up on her.'

'I've worked with the stuck-up little cow,' Diana said calmly. 'Trust me, you're better off without her.'

'And I chose Indira because I knew her career needed a boost,' said June. 'Her last book was remaindered, and no one wanted her on morning television any more. I always like to have one guest who's so desperate I can be sure they'll do anything I say.'

'You utter cow,' said Toby.

'I'm a professional,' said June. 'Which is more than I can say for you.'

'Back off,' said Diana, scowling fiercely at both of them. 'We have more important things to worry about.'

They all sat quietly for a while. Nobody looked at anybody else. The hall was so quiet they could hear each other breathing.

'There must be something we can do to protect ourselves!' Toby said finally.

'I already talked to the director,' said June. 'And told him to call the police. They'll be waiting outside once the locks open.'

'I wouldn't count on that,' said Alistair. 'You can't afford to assume there definitely is someone on the other end of the cameras.'

Everyone stared at him. This was a new idea, and they really
didn't like it.

'The technology always works perfectly on my show!' said
June. 'Because the technicians know what I'd do to them if
it didn't.'

'Trust me, they know,' Leslie said solemnly. 'There's not
one of them would dare fail her.'

'Then why aren't the phones working?' said Diana.

'That's nothing to do with me,' said June.

'Then what are we going to do?' said Toby. 'Just sit around
until the doors open, and hope we don't all die before then?'

'I know some good word games,' said Diana. 'You do a lot
of sitting around during filming.'

'We go on with the show,' said June.

'Are you kidding?' Toby said loudly. 'After everything that's
happened?'

'Especially after what's happened,' said June. 'Our audience
must be glued to their sets, waiting to see what will happen
next.'

Toby turned suddenly to face Leslie. 'You're the medium
on this show. Can't you get in touch with Indira, and ask her
what happened?'

'It doesn't work like that,' said Leslie.

'Imagine my surprise,' said Diana.

Toby stared implacably at Leslie. 'Try.'

The medium nodded slowly. 'Why not? The show must
go on.'

He arranged himself fussily, before closing his eyes and
steadying his breathing. Bit by bit, all the character seemed
to drop out of his face, until it was as blank as a mask. He
turned his head slowly back and forth, as though listening for
something. Alistair glanced quickly round the group. They
were all watching Leslie intently; not necessarily convinced,
but fascinated to see what he would do. Leslie sat very still,
and then his mouth dropped open. He made a few vague
sounds, like a radio trying to find a station, and then suddenly
he was speaking with Indira's voice.

'It's all right, Toby. You mustn't worry. I'm fine now. Daddy
was here, waiting for me.'

Toby looked as though he'd been hit.

'Indira?'

'I'm right here, Toby.'

'Who killed you?' said Toby, fighting to keep the pain out of his voice so he could speak clearly. 'Did you see who it was?'

'No. I was asleep; and then I woke up here. But Toby . . . You have to be careful. You all do. This isn't over yet . . .'

Leslie's mouth snapped shut, and his eyes flew open. He looked confused, and his face was wet with sweat. He shook himself hard, and then took out a handkerchief and mopped at his face.

'My gift is back,' he said slowly. 'After all this time, I've been forgiven . . .' He looked at Toby. 'There's a new ghost in the hall . . .'

'I don't believe you,' said Toby. But he didn't sound too sure about that.

'Leslie and I did have a discussion earlier on,' said Alistair. 'About an unseen extra presence he'd felt in the hall.'

'Really?' said Diana. 'When was this? And why didn't you share this information with the rest of us? I'm sure we'd have been absolutely fascinated.'

'We're talking about it now,' said Alistair.

'Then feel free to share with the group, darling,' said Diana.

'There were six of us, then,' Alistair said carefully. 'But Leslie was convinced he could sense a seventh, unseen, presence.'

'Who was it?' said Toby.

'Which part of *unseen* presence are you having problems with?' said Alistair.

Toby switched his glare to Leslie. 'Why didn't you tell us this before?'

'Because I didn't want you freaking out, like you are now,' said the medium.

'Can you sense this presence now?' said Alistair.

Diana leaned in close, to murmur in his ear. 'Don't encourage him. I keep telling you; it's all an act.'

'Right up to when it isn't,' said Alistair. 'Now hush, please; I want to hear what he has to say.'

Leslie took a deep breath, and looked slowly round the hall. His gaze was very intent, piercing the shadows as though they couldn't hope to hide any secrets from him. And then his breath caught in his throat, and he shuddered suddenly.

'There's a new presence here. I can feel it.'

'Indira?' said Toby.

'No,' said Leslie. 'It isn't human.'

Everyone sat up straight in their chairs, and looked at each other. The game had just changed, and not in a good way.

'Then what is it?' said Diana.

'Death,' said Leslie. 'Death has come among us. And you have no defence against it.' His head came up sharply. 'It's old, so old . . . A thing of hate, and horror!'

'Talk to us, Leslie,' said Alistair. 'Describe what it is you're seeing.'

The medium stood up so suddenly his chair toppled over backwards. 'It's coming right at us! Everyone on your feet! Form a circle! Shoulder to shoulder, looking outwards! Hurry! Your lives, your souls, depend on it!'

They were all out of their chairs now, compelled by the sheer terror in the medium's voice. They moved quickly to form a circle, shoulder pressing hard against shoulder as they stared around them, straining their eyes against the shadows. Alistair concentrated until his forehead ached, but still couldn't see or feel anything.

'Everyone hold hands to complete the circle,' said Leslie. 'Don't let go, for any reason. We have to keep it out . . .'

'Keep what out?' said Diana.

'The demon . . .' said Leslie.

Everyone grabbed someone's hand. They were all breathing hard, their heads whipping back and forth as they searched the gloom for an enemy. Diana gripped Alistair's hand painfully hard. Leslie's eyes bulged, and the veins stood out on his forehead. His gaze moved jerkily round the hall, as though tracking something as it moved around the circle.

'What are you seeing?' said Alistair.

'It's so old . . .' said the medium, his voice little more than a whisper. 'Older than the hall, older than the town . . .' His gaze came to a halt, apparently fixed on something right in front of him. His voice dropped to a whisper. 'What are you?'

Alistair still couldn't see anything. All he could feel was Diana gripping his hand like a drowning woman going down for the third time; and Toby's hand, trembling with tension and wet with sweat. June had her eyes shut, refusing to see anything. Leslie looked lost, not sure what to do. And Alistair knew it was down to him. He raised his voice, struggling to make it sound calm and assured.

'I invoke God's protection. In his name, let no evil thing enter in here.'

His voice resounded across the hall, loud and carrying and full of conviction. And then Leslie let out a long ragged breath.

'It's going away . . . It's retreating . . . It's gone. I can't feel its presence any more.'

He seemed to collapse in on himself, and all but fell back into his chair. Slowly, everyone in the circle let go of each other's hands, and looked shakily about them. Diana turned to Alistair, beaming all over her face.

'That was incredible, darling! You drove it away!'

'Any power came from God, not from me,' said Alistair.

'Oh shut up and take a compliment,' said Diana.

She threw her arms around Alistair and hugged him fiercely, and he held her to him. But still, he couldn't help wondering why he hadn't been able to feel any presence at all . . .

SIX
Noises Off

A fter a while, Alistair leaned back a little and smiled at Diana.

'You know, we have been holding on to each other for quite a while now. People will talk.'

'That's their problem,' Diana said comfortably. 'They're just jealous. Let them get their own bishop.'

'This is going somewhere, isn't it?' said Alistair.

'If you're lucky,' said Diana.

She gave him one last squeeze, hard enough to drive the breath out of any man who hadn't been an athlete at Oxford, and then pushed Alistair away. They then stood side by side, cool and composed, as they looked around the hall. It seemed peaceful enough, and reassuringly quiet. June and Leslie were muttering together, as usual, while Toby stood alone, staring around him as though daring anything to sneak up on him.

'Well,' Alistair said finally. 'All that "Stand in a circle and see off the Devil" stuff was all very interesting, I suppose. But I have to ask: what the hell was that all about?'

'Don't ask me, darling,' said Diana. 'I was there when it happened, and I'm still not sure. You're supposed to be our expert on things beyond our ken, so if you haven't a clue, I couldn't even venture an uneducated guess. All I know for sure is that when it mattered, you stepped up to bat and saved us all.'

'Perhaps,' said Alistair. 'I'm still not certain that anything I did made any real difference.'

'You drove off a demon through an act of faith,' said Leslie, coming over to join them. 'I have to say, Bishop, I'm impressed.'

'A demon?' said Alistair. 'Is that what we're calling it?'

Leslie looked at him curiously. 'Something vicious from

the dark places, a terrible presence from the underworld, a
threat to our very souls . . . What else would you call it?'

'Let me get back to you on that,' said Alistair.

He nodded courteously to Diana, and moved away. He felt
a need to be on his own, with his own thoughts. He was having
trouble making up his mind as to what he'd actually experienced. His life as a bishop in one of London's high-crime
parishes, followed by an entirely unexpected second career in
morning television, had done nothing to prepare him for an
open attack by an infernal power. If that was what had actually happened. It disturbed Alistair how quickly he and
everyone else had come to believe in an invisible threat,
and put their faith in a defensive circle, just because they were
under the influence of a show-biz medium.

It had certainly seemed real enough at the time, with
everyone driven along by the sheer terror and urgency in
Leslie's voice. But now, considering it all in the peace and
quiet of a perfectly empty hall, Alistair wasn't sure he believed
any of it. Not least because he was having serious trouble
believing he had the spiritual authority to dismiss a demon
with just a few words. Technically, as a representative of his
church, of course he had that power; but he couldn't help
feeling there ought to be more to it than that. But then he was
pulled out of his reverie by raised voices, and when he looked
round, Diana was glaring right into Leslie's face.

'What was a demon from hell doing in a small country town
hall?'

'I've been wondering that too,' said Leslie. Doing his best
not to appear too intimidated by the scowling presence before
him. 'I can only assume something must have happened, to
draw the demon here.'

'Like what?' said Diana.

'Damned if I know,' said Leslie, with disarming candour.
'I can't think of anything in the old stories that would explain
what just happened.'

Toby suddenly turned his head to look at them, and something very like his old smile tugged at his mouth.

'Maybe the local townswomen's guild have been practising
a little devil worship on the sly. You know, cavorting in the

buff and dancing for the devil, before getting down to some good old-fashioned group sex. There's not a lot to do for entertainment in small country towns like this.'

Leslie managed a brief smile of his own. 'I'm sure I would have stumbled across some gossip about that kind of thing, while I was doing my research. All I found were records of craft fairs, whist drives, and regular get-togethers for people with bad legs.'

Diana turned away with an exasperated sound, and looked to Alistair for support.

'What do you think, Bish? Do you believe in demons?'

Alistair spread his hands helplessly. 'My religion requires that I believe in such things; but I honestly never thought I would end up face to face with such a thing. Even if, strictly speaking, it didn't have a face.' He studied Leslie carefully. 'You're the only one who saw what was threatening us. Can you describe it?'

'I only experienced it with my inner eye,' said Leslie. 'It was more like an impression . . . Of darkness made manifest, walking in the world with bad intent.'

He broke off, to think about that. Everyone waited politely, but he had nothing more to say.

'All very dramatic, I'm sure,' Diana said finally. 'If you ever get tired of being a medium, I can get you regular work doing horror audiobooks. But as descriptions of demonic presences go, I'd have to say that wasn't particularly helpful.'

Alistair raised his voice, to get Leslie's attention. 'You snapped into action pretty quickly, for a support host on a television show. Have you encountered this kind of thing before?'

Leslie shook his head. 'Never. And I'm really hoping I won't have to again.'

Toby looked at him sharply. 'Are you saying there's a chance that thing might be back?'

'I don't know,' said Leslie. 'How could I? This is all new territory to me. I'm just a medium; I deal in restless spirits and the unquiet dead . . . Not direct threats from infernal powers!'

'Leave the man alone!' June came striding forward,

advancing on the group like a warship under full sail. 'He doesn't know anything. He never does. And he's clearly in shock.'

Alistair stared unflinchingly into her furious gaze. 'You said you didn't believe in the supernatural. But you were quick enough to join hands and make yourself part of the defensive circle.'

'All hands to the pump when the ship is sinking,' June said briskly. 'And, no atheists in spiritual foxholes.' She nodded approvingly to Leslie. 'You put on a really good performance, for once. Very convincing. Should get us some excellent viewing figures.'

Diana frowned. 'Are you saying you only went along with it because you thought it would look good?'

June smirked. 'Demons, my arse. You just scared each other into a shared delusion.'

'But if the demon is real,' Toby said slowly, 'maybe Leslie could use his medium skills to call it back.'

Diana looked at him disbelievingly. 'Why would we want to do that?'

'Because it must know things, about what's really going on here,' said Toby. 'With Leslie's skills, and the power of Alistair's faith, maybe we could make it talk.'

Leslie was so taken aback by the prospect that he actually spluttered for a moment, before he could get any words out.

'Are you out of your mind?' he said finally. 'We were lucky to survive what just happened. You have no idea how lucky.'

Toby stared coldly at the medium, not giving an inch. 'Could this demon have been involved in Indira's death?'

'It's possible, I suppose,' said Leslie, with the air of someone leaning over backwards to be scrupulously fair. 'But even if you could persuade me to try and summon that thing back, which I'm pretty sure you couldn't, I don't know of any way to compel it to speak the truth.'

'Let us all be very clear on this,' Alistair said firmly. 'Under no circumstances are we to even try calling back a demon from Hell. On the grounds that we are not insanely stupid.'

Toby scowled, and thought hard.

Leslie nodded to Alistair. 'Thank you. It's good to know we have one sensible voice in the group.'

'On the other hand . . .' said Toby.

'Oh, what now?' said the medium.

'Back before all the crazy stuff started,' Toby said slowly, 'Indira spoke to me through you. So, Leslie . . . put on your medium's hat, and call her back. Let's see if she can tell us what's going on here.'

'I have no power over Indira's spirit,' said Leslie. 'I didn't summon her. She just arrived.'

'If she came to you once, she can do it again!' said Toby. 'Just . . . reach out to her!'

'You don't know what you're asking!' said Leslie.

'Bring her back!' said Toby.

He headed straight for the medium, his face full of a cold, implacable determination. Leslie backed away, and Toby went after him. Alistair stepped quickly forward, and placed himself between the two men. Toby stopped, because it was either that or walk right through Alistair; and, angry as he was, Toby still knew better than to try that. Alistair raised both his hands placatingly, while keeping his voice carefully calm and moderate.

'We're in a bad situation, Toby. Let's not make things worse.'

'Get out of my way,' said Toby.

'That's not going to happen,' said Alistair. 'Please, Toby; think what you're doing. Indira wouldn't want this.'

'Stop saying that!'

The punch Toby threw had enough strength in it to really make a mess of Alistair's face. But Alistair just ducked to one side at the last moment, and let the blow sail harmlessly over his shoulder. He then grabbed hold of Toby's arm while he was off balance, and twisted it painfully. Toby cried out as the leverage bent him forward until he was facing the floor. Sweat dripped from his straining features as he struggled to break free, but he only hurt himself more. Toby cried out again, in pain and frustration. Diana started to protest, but broke off as Alistair shot her a sharp, unflinching gaze. He looked down at Toby, and when he spoke his voice was still perfectly calm and measured.

'We are in a very difficult situation, Toby; and you're not helping. I need you to calm down, so you can help us figure out what's going on. Hopefully, that will include discovering who hurt Indira. There are no short cuts we can trust, and that includes a medium we can't be certain is on our side. Now, I'm going to let you go and step back . . . And you are going to save your anger for the real enemy. Keep a lid on it, Toby. Do it for Indira.'

He let go, and moved away. Toby slowly straightened up and massaged his aching shoulder. He looked at Alistair, who was clearly ready to go another round if that was what was needed. Everyone watched them silently. Toby finally nodded, all the anger gone from his face.

'I'm sorry. It's just . . . I miss her so much.'

'Of course you do,' said Alistair.

Toby walked away, not looking at anyone, and Alistair let him go. Diana slipped in beside him.

'That was pretty full on, Bish.'

'I didn't want to hurt him,' said Alistair. 'He's been hurt so much already. But if we start fighting each other, we might never get out of here alive.'

Diana shot a quick glance at June. 'Our gracious host actually looks disappointed that it didn't all descend into harsh man-on-man action.'

'I caught a glimpse of her face, while I was handling Toby,' said Alistair. 'She seemed to be enjoying the spectacle. And hoping it would get out of hand, so she'd have a big dramatic scene to entertain her audience.'

'There's something very wrong with that woman,' said Diana. 'There are more important things in life than putting on a good show and playing to the camera, and yes, I am aware of the irony in me saying that.'

June came striding over to join them. She planted herself in front of Alistair and looked him over.

'You're very good with your hands, Bishop. You put Toby in his place without even breaking a sweat.' She shot a quick look at Diana. 'I'm sure he's extremely huggable, dear, but don't you wonder if he might put you in a choke hold, if he thought you were causing a problem?'

Diana smiled at June; and it wasn't a nice smile. 'You do love to stir things up, don't you? Always ready to create some trouble if there isn't any, to entertain your viewers. We were just attacked by a demon from hell! Wasn't that dramatic enough for you?'

June shrugged. 'Watching people stare wide-eyed at something that isn't there won't help maintain the viewing figures. All the audience will have seen is a group of people having hysterics. I prefer to go with what I know they like – emotional fireworks between the guests.' She turned back to Alistair. 'You're doing an excellent job riding herd on the group, Bishop; but I have to wonder just how far you would go to keep the peace. When the calm and reasonable words clearly aren't working, but you still have to make people behave?'

Alistair met her gaze calmly. 'There wouldn't be so much tension, if you didn't keep stoking the flames and pouring on gasoline.'

'Are you threatening me, Alistair?' said June, her eyes sparkling. 'Are you getting ready to lay hands on me?'

'Don't fall for that one, Bish,' said Diana. 'She'd probably enjoy it.'

Alistair fixed June with a cold stare. 'I am about to change the subject, and you are going to go along with it; because if you don't, I will tear every single camera out of the walls, throw them on the ground and stamp on them.'

June looked genuinely shocked. 'You wouldn't!'

Alistair couldn't keep a smile off his face. 'Try me.'

'Oh very well then, change your damned subject,' said June, not quite pouting. 'See if I care.'

Alistair looked at Leslie and Toby, and cleared his throat loudly to get their attention.

'Please come over and join us, gentlemen. We have important matters to discuss.'

'Just what we need,' Toby muttered, as he and Leslie rejoined the group. 'A discussion group. Maybe we could follow it up with a jamboree and a singalong.'

Alistair ignored him, and concentrated his gaze on June. 'I think it's time for you to tell us the true history of this hall.

But I only want to hear about the weird things that actually happened here.'

'Ask Leslie,' June said immediately. 'He's the one who knows all this stuff, because he does all the research. I just pick out the best bits, and assemble them into something we can build on.'

'When you don't simply make it all up,' said Leslie.

'We are not in the documentary business!' said June.

'Just the facts, Leslie,' said Alistair.

The medium nodded uncomfortably. 'Most of the stories you heard earlier were only tall tales and scare stories spread by the locals.' He stopped and frowned, gathering his thoughts. 'There have always been stories, about the hall. Nothing particularly dramatic, and rarely anything specific. Just . . . stories.

'Nothing ever happens during the day, or when the hall is occupied; it's always after dark, when the hall is locked up and supposed to be empty. And never anything traditional; nothing you'd expect. No ghostly figures walking through the walls, or lurking in the shadows. Never any sightings, or manifestations . . . Mostly it's just a mood, an atmosphere, a feeling of something not right. Unexpected lights at the windows, strange voices from inside the hall . . . But when people go inside to investigate, there's never anyone there.'

'Then how did this place end up being labelled the most haunted hall in England?' said Diana.

Leslie smiled condescendingly. 'Because that was what the townspeople wanted. They made up the right kind of ghost stories to bring in the tourists, and the money they spend. But the tourist boom didn't last long; there was too much competition from other towns with better stories and more interesting histories. And a lot of the visitors didn't care for the atmosphere around the hall, even during the day . . . That's why the town council was so happy for us to hire this place; they want us to find out what's wrong, and do something about it. Because they think we're for real.'

'We are for real,' said June. 'We just pander to people who believe in stuff that isn't.'

'So why fill your advance publicity with all the made-up stories?' said Diana.

June smiled patronizingly. 'Because that's show business, darling. Feed the audience what they want and they'll eat it up with spoons. And come back for more.'

'Season after season,' said Leslie.

'How can you still not believe, after everything we've been through?' said Toby.

'I haven't seen anything,' June said stubbornly.

'There were times when you seemed just as freaked out as the rest of us,' said Diana.

'I was being in the moment,' said June. 'And if I did occasionally feel something . . . That was probably nothing more than group hysteria.'

'The twenty-seven people who died in this hall were real enough,' said Leslie. 'And the woman who vanished from the dressing room. She was a real person, with a life and a family, but her disappearance was never solved. I suppose her friends could have made the whole thing up, but why would they?

'The locals have been telling the same stories for years, about uneasy feelings, strange things they've seen and heard, and a sense of being watched by unseen eyes. That's why June and I chose this setting for our big comeback; because we could build anything we wanted on stories so vague.'

'That's a bit cold-blooded, isn't it?' said Toby.

Leslie smiled. 'Have you met June?'

Alistair fixed his attention on her. 'You still haven't made it clear why you chose us to be your guests. I get that you couldn't get the star turns you really wanted, but you didn't just pick our names out of a hat. You must have seen something in us that you could turn to your advantage.'

'You've all reported encounters with the supernatural,' June said flatly.

'I didn't know that,' said Toby.

'Indira mentioned in several interviews that she often talked with her deceased grandmother,' said Leslie. 'And got some of her best recipes from her.' He paused, and looked round the group. 'Feel free to tell your own stories, if you'd find that more comfortable.'

They all looked at each other. In the end, Toby shrugged heavily.

'I suppose I might as well go first. An old friend of mine died on stage, right in the middle of his act. Got a really big laugh, until the audience realized. Some time later, I was booked into the same theatre, and ended up in the same dressing room he used. And on my first night there I looked into the makeup mirror and, instead of my own reflection . . . I saw his face staring back at me.

'He was screaming silently, his bulging eyes fixed on mine, as though he was desperately trying to warn me about something. I backed away from the mirror, right across the room, until I slammed up against the far wall. He never once took his gaze off me. I squeezed my eyes shut, and when I opened them again, he was gone. Nothing in the mirror but my own reflection. I cancelled the gig and walked out. The story turned up in the media when the theatre management tried to sue me.'

'Did you ever find out what your friend was trying to warn you about?' said Diana.

'No,' said Toby. 'I never saw him again. Hopefully by leaving the theatre when I did, I dodged whatever bullet fate had in store for me. Unless he was trying to warn me not to come on this show.'

'I've never understood why supernatural warnings have to be so vague,' said Diana. 'Why can't they take the time to get the details right?' She turned to Alistair. 'Your turn, darling. What happened to you?'

'Nothing ghostly, or even supernatural, technically speaking,' said Alistair. 'I had a near-death experience. I've talked about it several times on television.'

'I never watch morning shows,' said Diana. 'I have self-respect.'

'You've appeared on enough of them,' said June.

'That's different,' said Diana. 'It's part of the job.'

Alistair cleared his throat, and everyone turned back to him.

'I was in hospital, to have some wisdom teeth taken out under a general anaesthetic, but something went wrong. When I finally woke up, I remembered floating up by the ceiling, watching my body convulse on the table while a whole bunch of really worried-looking professionals tried every trick they knew to drag me back from the brink.

'Afterwards, I talked to the hospital officials about my experience, and even described some of the extreme measures I'd seen the doctors using, and the officials declared it must have been some kind of delusion, caused by oxygen starvation to the brain. But privately, several members of staff admitted to me that they'd heard similar stories from other patients. What bothers me is that I didn't see any of the usual things. No bright light, no tunnel leading to the hereafter . . . I would have liked some evidence that there really is a better place waiting.'

'But you're in the faith business,' said Toby. 'Perhaps you're not allowed anything that might affect that faith.'

'Or perhaps it was all just a dream,' said Alistair. 'Not a good ending to a story, I know.' He turned to Diana.

'I had my own near-death experience,' she said slowly. 'Though perhaps appropriately, mine was rather more dramatic. I was appearing in the West End, in *Nosferatu, The Musical*, and we were using a lot of old-fashioned stage tricks to bolster the mood. Including trapdoors and puffs of smoke, so the vampires could appear and disappear. But one evening a trapdoor opened when it shouldn't have, and I happened to be standing on it. I fell quite a way, and suffered severe head injuries.'

She paused, frowning.

'I remember standing at the foot of a gangway, leading up to a massive cruise liner getting ready to depart. It was a bright summer's day, under a perfect blue sky. I was just about to go on board when a purser suddenly appeared, and told me my ticket was invalid. So I could only stand there and watch as the ship sailed away . . . And I felt sad, so sad . . .'

'I think the key words here are: severe head injuries,' said Toby.

'Whatever floats your boat, darling,' said Diana.

Alistair smiled at her. 'You saw everything I would have liked to. I think I'm jealous.'

Diana smiled back at him. 'Some day your ship will come.'

Alistair turned to June. 'You thought our experiences would make us more . . . suggestible?'

'Something like that,' said June.

'Exactly like that,' said Leslie.

'That is really cold,' said Toby.

'You didn't think I chose you for your personalities, did you?' said June.

'You know,' said Leslie, 'I can remember when you had charm.'

'I can remember when you weren't a liability,' said June.

'Knock it off!' Diana said loudly. She glared around the group. 'We're all under a lot of pressure, and the only way we're going to get through this is if we work together. So instead of all this endless bickering and getting on each other's nerves, can I suggest we concentrate on finding a way out of this place!'

'What did you have in mind?' said Toby. 'Dig a tunnel?'

'There has to be some way!' said Diana.

'But there isn't,' said June.

'You can't be sure of that,' said Alistair.

'I'm afraid she can,' said Leslie. 'June and I put a lot of thought into making sure no one could leave. That was one of the main selling points for the show.'

'For the drama,' said June, in the tone of someone who was getting really tired of having to make the same point over and over again. 'The doors can't be opened, and the windows are far too narrow for any of us to squeeze through.'

They all took a moment to study the tall thin windows, and then nod reluctantly.

'We could smash the glass,' Toby said tentatively. 'And then throw out a note, asking for help.'

'We're on television!' June said crushingly. 'The whole world can see we're trapped. It wouldn't surprise me if the entire car park was packed full of police, fire services, and rescue equipment . . . But the only way they could get to us would be to smash a hole through one of the walls; and given that the time-locks will open anyway in a few hours, it makes more sense for them to just be patient and wait. As far as they're concerned, we're in no immediate danger.'

'But we are!' said Diana.

'I doubt any of the authorities will take our demonic attack seriously,' said Leslie. 'It's far more likely they'll think it's part of the show, and applaud our acting skills. Face it, people, we're on our own.'

'If we were, I wouldn't feel so worried,' said Diana.

Toby suddenly brightened, as a thought struck him. He grinned quickly at Alistair.

'I saw something useful, in the kitchen.'

He hurried over to the side door, disappeared through it, and then after a moment came back out carrying a heavy red fire extinguisher.

'Just the job!' he said proudly.

'What use is that?' said Diana. 'Unless you're suggesting we set fire to the main doors, smash them down once they're weakened, and then use the extinguisher to hold back the flames while we make our escape?'

Toby looked at her. 'Actually, that's not a bad idea. As a last resort. No, I was thinking that this thing is big and heavy enough to batter down those doors, if I really put my back into it.'

Leslie was already shaking his head.

'Our security people put a lot of work into reinforcing those doors. They assured me you could drive a car right into them, and the only damage would be to the car.'

'And given how much they charged us, I believe them,' said June.

'Anyone would think you don't want us to get out of here,' said Toby.

He hefted the fire extinguisher manfully, and carried it over to the main doors.

'Oh to hell with it!' June yelled after him. 'You go, Toby! Smash those doors down! You can do it!'

'No he can't,' said Leslie. 'Come on, June, we talked about this.'

'Keep the noise down, Leslie,' said June, not even glancing at him. 'This will make for great television, whether he succeeds or not.'

Toby raised the extinguisher with both hands, and slammed its base against the solid wood. There was a loud thud, and the doors jumped and shuddered, but they didn't give. Toby hammered the extinguisher against the doors again and again,

but the wood didn't so much as crack. Toby began to gasp
and groan from the effort he was putting into every blow.
Sweat poured down his face. His arms trembled from the
strain, but he wouldn't let himself be beaten. June was still
yelling encouragement. Diana put a concerned hand on
Alistair's arm. He nodded quickly, and turned to June.

'Stop that. Right now.'

'I'm helping him!' said June.

'No,' said Alistair. 'You aren't.'

She took in the expression on his face, and stopped yelling.
Alistair went over to join Toby before the main doors. The
fire extinguisher was resting on the floor, with Toby bent over
it. His face was a flushed, unhealthy colour, and he was struggling to get his breath. He wouldn't even look at Alistair, as
he started to raise the extinguisher again.

'That's enough, Toby,' said Alistair. 'You've done all you
can. It was a good idea, but those doors are never going to
cooperate.'

Toby was breathing so hard he couldn't even answer Alistair.
He fought to lift the extinguisher high enough for another
blow. Gently but firmly, Alistair took it away from him. Toby
almost collapsed, without his obsession to hold him up. Alistair
knew better than to try and support him. He had to allow Toby
his pride. He put the extinguisher down, and leaned it against
the doors. Toby waited for his breathing to settle, and then
glared at Alistair.

'Why did you have to interfere?'

'Because you're not doing any damage,' said Alistair.
'Except to your heart.'

'Are you going to let him talk to you like that?' yelled June,
her eyes bright and eager.

'Oh shut up, you vicious little cow,' said Diana. She drove
an elbow into June's ribs, and the producer gasped and bent
over. Diana sniffed coldly. 'You were only encouraging Toby
in the hope he'd have some kind of heart problem, because
that would be good for the show!'

June straightened up, hiding her pain behind a professional
face. 'The fire extinguisher was Toby's idea. I was just being
supportive.'

'You're not fooling anyone,' said Diana.

Toby glared at Alistair. 'I'm fine. I can handle pressure. I do live comedy, remember? I don't need you to hold my hand.'

The fact that he was still having to force the words out past his strained breathing rather undermined his argument, but Alistair didn't say anything. Toby finally sighed, and managed the ghost of a smile.

'You can keep the extinguisher.'

He walked away, not even glancing back at the doors. June started to say something, but Diana pulled back her elbow and June changed her mind. Alistair gave the door handles a hopeful rattle, just in case, but the locks remained stubbornly defiant. Alistair turned away to find June was talking quietly with Leslie. They were both checking their watches, and comparing the time. Which seemed a little odd under the circumstances. Alistair had to wonder when he became so suspicious and cynical, and then smiled as he realized he already knew the answer. When he became a part of this show. He moved over to join June and Leslie.

'What's so important about the time?' he said. 'Is there somewhere you have to be?'

Both hosts showed him their most professional smile.

'So much has been happening, I lost track of the time,' said June.

'It's always later than you think,' said Leslie.

'Yes, thank you, Leslie,' said June. 'I know I can always rely on you to be no support at all.'

'That's what I'm here for,' said Leslie.

'Hey, Bishop!' Toby called out. 'Do you think you could come over here?'

Alistair gave June and Leslie his best hard look, to make it clear they hadn't fooled him for a moment, and then walked over to Toby, who was leaning heavily on one of the chairs.

'How are you feeling?'

'Like an idiot,' said Toby. 'You couldn't get through those doors with a steam-powered battering ram.' He looked across at June. 'Did she really just try to encourage me into another heart attack?'

'Wouldn't surprise me one bit,' said Alistair. 'I think that woman would do absolutely anything to make this show a success.'

A series of loud knocking noises suddenly rang out in the hall. Alistair stared quickly around him, trying to figure out where the sounds were coming from. Toby stood up straight, and gestured at the doors.

'Could that be the police, or the fire services, trying to get to us?'

'The sounds are coming from the walls, not the doors!' said June.

The knockings grew louder, like someone demanding to be let in. Or something ready to break down the walls to get to them. Diana moved in quickly beside Alistair and Toby.

'What the hell is that?'

'It's a bit loud to be a water hammer,' said Toby.

'Where exactly are the sounds coming from?' said Diana, swivelling her head back and forth.

'From outside,' said Leslie.

'Outside where?' said Diana.

'Everything,' said Leslie.

'OK . . .' said Toby. 'Somebody has seriously lost the plot.'

Alistair stabbed a finger at the far end of the hall. 'The knockings seem to be coming from the wall behind the stage.'

Everyone turned to look. Toby nodded his head judiciously.

'Damn, you've got good ears. Any idea what it is we're hearing?'

'Something is trying to get our attention,' said Leslie. 'And not in a good way.'

'Who's that knock-knock-knocking at my door . . .?' said Diana.

'No one is to say or even think the words "Come in",' said Alistair, very firmly.

'How about if we all shout "Piss off!" really loudly?' said Toby.

Diana glared at him. 'You honestly think it's a good idea to upset someone who can knock that loudly?'

The knockings seemed to move slowly along the far wall

until they reached the end, and then transferred themselves to the side wall, and progressed slowly along that.

'Who the hell is knocking?' said Toby.

'Something not of this world,' said Leslie.

'Why would anything like that need to knock?' Diana said scathingly. 'The demon didn't bother to announce itself; it just came straight at us.'

'There's a lot going on in this hall,' said Leslie.

Diana saw something in Alistair's face, and moved in closer. 'You've thought of something. What is it?'

'These knockings remind me of the footsteps we heard earlier,' he said slowly. 'Sounds designed to frighten . . . But if you listen carefully, although the knocks are getting really loud, none of them echo. Which should be impossible, in a hall this large . . .'

'You thought the footsteps might have a natural explanation,' said Diana, hanging on to common sense with both hands. 'Old wood, contracting and expanding. Could this be more of the same?'

'This is too loud to be anything natural,' said Alistair. 'It feels more like an attack . . .'

The knockings moved slowly along the wall, crossed the side door, and kept going.

'They're heading towards us,' Diana said tightly.

'Miners often hear knockings when they're alone in the dark, in the deepest parts of a mine,' said Toby. 'It's supposed to come from miners killed in a cave-in, still desperately signalling for help . . .'

Diana glared at him. 'Miners? In a town hall? Seriously?'

'The knockings are heading for the main doors!' June shouted.

Diana turned quickly to Alistair. 'We can't let them get in! Should we barricade the doors?'

'Since we couldn't get out,' said Alistair. 'I don't see how anything could get in.'

'Stop being reasonable, and do something!' said Diana.

'Maybe we should invite it in?' said Toby. 'Be friendly?'

'Does that sound like anything we should invite in?' said Leslie.

'All right, bad idea,' said Toby. 'Forget I mentioned it.'
June clapped both hands over her ears. 'I can't stand loud noises! Somebody make it stop!'
Leslie put an arm across her shoulders, but she shrugged it away. Toby advanced on the main doors, his fists raised.
'Show yourself, you bastard! I'm not afraid of you!'
'Really not a good idea!' said Leslie.
'Stay away from the doors, Toby!' said Alistair. 'The sounds are just trying to frighten us into doing something stupid.'
'We have to do something,' said Toby, not taking his eyes off the doors.
'I know,' said Alistair. 'But doing the wrong thing could put us all at risk.'
Toby nodded reluctantly, and backed away from the doors. Diana grabbed urgently at Alistair's arm.
'Say the words again! The ones that drove off the demon!'
'I'm not sure the words did anything,' said Alistair. 'I'm not even sure there was a demon. Leslie was the only one who saw it.'
'I found him very convincing,' said Diana.
'All good actors are,' said Alistair.
Diana looked at him, so startled she forgot all about the knockings.
'Are you saying he made the whole thing up?'
'I didn't see or sense a thing,' said Alistair. 'But the defensive circle did make for really good television . . .'
'Hey!' said Toby, glowering fiercely. 'Something really powerful is doing its best to batter down the walls! A little practical help and assistance would not go unappreciated!'
'They're just sounds!' said Alistair.
Toby shook his head disgustedly. 'And denial isn't just a river in Egypt. By not believing what's right in front of us, you're the one who's putting us in danger.'
'He could be right,' said Diana. 'We might not understand what's happening, but we still have to deal with it.'
'But are the sounds really real?' Alistair said stubbornly. Suddenly it seemed vitally important for him to convince someone that what he was saying made sense. 'Everything that's happening seems designed to put the wind up us!'

'We are moments away from a close encounter of the infernal kind, and you want to spend your last few minutes playing guessing games?' Leslie said loudly. 'Are you out of your mind?'

He came hurrying over to confront Alistair. June stuck close beside him. She'd taken her hands away from her ears, but didn't look at all happy about it.

'All right,' said Alistair. 'This is me, being reasonable. If you have something to say, I'll listen.'

'There has to be some purpose behind all of this,' Leslie said steadily. 'The footsteps seemed to be heading toward something, and the knockings want to get in. The demon threatened us. There must be something in this hall that's attracting attention from beyond the fields we know.'

'Like what?' said Diana. 'We've been all over the hall, and didn't find a thing!'

'Maybe it wants one of us,' said June.

'It can have you,' said Toby.

June ignored him, her gaze fixed on Alistair. 'You drove the demon away. Do it again.'

'There's no real threat!' said Alistair.

'There could be, once it gets in . . .' said Leslie.

'You saved us before,' said June. 'Do it again. Say the words.'

Alistair glared at her. 'You just want me to put on a show for your audience.'

'Why are you being so difficult?' said Leslie.

'That is a good question, Alistair,' said Diana.

Because I don't think I believe any of this, thought Alistair. But he couldn't bring himself to say it out loud.

Toby gestured at the main doors. 'The knockings are getting louder. How long do you think those doors will hold, against something not of this world?'

Alistair gestured angrily. 'Look at the doors! Something is hammering away, fit to raise the dead, but the doors aren't shaking at all! Even though they did when you pounded at them with the extinguisher.'

The knockings suddenly stopped. They didn't slow down, or fade away; there was just a terribly loud and threatening knock, and then nothing to follow it. The hall was very still and very quiet. Everyone stood close together, looking uncertainly about them . . . And then, one by one, they slowly relaxed, and let out breaths they hadn't realized they'd been holding.

'It's over,' said Diana.

'For now,' said Leslie.

Toby looked reproachfully at Alistair. 'You should have said the words. If only to make sure whatever that was won't come back and try again.'

'Toby's right,' said Leslie. 'I think it would be in all our best interests if you were to perform an exorcism, and make this place safe from all outside threats.'

'I'm not convinced there are any,' said Alistair.

'What about Indira?' said Toby.

June nodded fiercely. 'Who else has to die, Bishop, to prove you wrong?'

SEVEN
Voices in the Dark

Everyone stared at Alistair, and he stared right back at them. His face remained completely calm and collected, and his gaze never wavered. He just stood his ground, not giving an inch. June and Leslie were the first to look away. The two hosts had only been interested in what they could push Alistair into; once it became clear he wasn't going to be pushed, they lost interest. Toby made an impatient sound, and jerked his gaze away. He'd already gone up against Alistair, and knew he couldn't win. Diana didn't look away, but the nature of her gaze slowly changed. She nodded slowly, and then smiled at Alistair, and he smiled back.

'You know I'm right,' said Alistair.

'I'm not sure about anything,' said Diana. 'But hey, it's you, Bish. So I'll go along. No exorcism it is. It's not like anyone here is spitting pea soup and spinning their head round. All I'm seeing is bad temper and borderline panic.'

'Understandable,' said Alistair. 'We've all been through a lot.'

Diana shot him a hard look. 'There is such a thing as being too understanding . . .'

Toby stomped over to join them, glowering self-consciously. 'Since the time-locks have us by the unmentionables, we're trapped in here with a whole bunch of weird phenomena that might or might not turn out to be the real thing, which we can't do anything about . . . So if an exorcism isn't on the table, let's concentrate on what we can do to fight back.'

'Did you have something in mind?' Alistair said politely.

Toby nodded at Leslie. 'I say we go for a full-on séance. See if we can make contact with whatever it is that's behind all this weird shit.' He quickly raised a hand, to forestall any questions or protestations. 'I don't care about the weirdness;

I just need to know who killed Indira. So I can do something about it.'

He looked at Alistair and Diana, and then at June and Leslie, to see how his suggestion was going down, and one by one they all nodded their agreement. Alistair didn't believe in séances any more than he did mediums, but he was curious to see what Leslie would do. The medium looked reproachfully at the rest of the group, as though they'd let him down by expecting too much of him. He nodded resignedly to Toby.

'What do you want me to do?'

'Find Indira again. Let her talk through you. If she doesn't know anything, contact anything else that's hanging around here. See if you can get some answers out of them.'

'I don't think you should expect too much in the way of actual information, Toby,' Alistair said carefully.

'Of course you don't,' said Toby. 'Because you refuse to believe the evidence of your own senses. Come on, Bishop: open your eyes, and pay attention! Weird Shit Central has broken out in this hall, and you're still burying your head in the sand. A distinct lack of faith from a man of the cloth.'

'I don't believe that any of the things we've been seeing, or hearing, are necessarily what we think they are,' said Alistair.

'That's your problem,' said Toby.

'Before we commit ourselves to something we can't take back,' said Leslie, 'can I just say . . .'

'No you can't,' said June. 'Get on with it.'

'Given how bad things already are,' Leslie said doggedly, 'do we really want to risk making them worse?'

Toby stabbed a finger at the main doors. 'Once those locks finally open, the police will come charging in. They'll take Indira away, and with her our last chance at solving this. I need to know who did it!' He took a moment, and everyone was careful to look somewhere else until he'd got his emotions under control. 'I need to hear Indira's voice again. I need to tell her I'm sorry, for not protecting her like I swore I would. And I need to promise her that whoever hurt her will be punished.' He took a deep breath, and nodded quickly to

Alistair. 'Yes, I know, I'm clutching at straws. But what else is there?'

Before Alistair could say anything, Diana cut in.

'You're quite right, Toby. We've tried being sensible and rational, and where has that got us? Up supernatural creek without a paddle. A séance could at least provide us with some idea of what we're facing. So let's do it. Fight fire with fire.'

Alistair looked at her. 'What makes you think we can trust anything that comes from June's pet medium?'

'I am standing right here,' said Leslie.

'We know,' Diana said crushingly.

Leslie pulled his dignity about him. 'I provide a bridge, between this world and the next. Not unlike you, Bishop. Except that I get tangible results.'

'We do usually put on a séance, at some point in the proceedings,' said June. 'The old voices from beyond bit always goes down well with the viewers.'

'I am not your performing seal,' said Leslie.

'You are whatever I say you are,' said June. 'And don't you forget it.'

Leslie sighed quietly, and looked out at the surrounding shadows.

'This isn't our show any more. We haven't been in control for some time now. The hall is generating actual supernatural phenomena, which means the threat to all of us is very real.'

'This is no time to lose your nerve,' said June.

Leslie turned suddenly, and glared at her with unexpected venom.

'Opening my mind under conditions like this would be like lighting a fire in a jungle clearing and then waiting to see which predators turn up.'

'Let them come,' said Toby. 'I'm really in the mood to beat the crap out of something.'

Diana smiled brightly at Alistair. 'And if violence and righteous fury aren't enough to see off the great unknown, we still have you to protect us. Like you did with the demon.'

'You shouldn't rely on a few words to keep you safe,' said Alistair.

'It was never about the words,' said Diana. 'I have faith in you.'

Alistair looked into Diana's eyes, and was touched by the confidence he found there.

'We have no idea of what's really going on here,' he said quietly.

'A séance could tell us,' said Diana.

'You can't really believe that,' said Alistair.

Diana snorted loudly. 'I'm ready to believe in anything that might help us sort this mess out.'

'That's the spirit,' said Toby.

June marched right up to Leslie, and stuck her face into his.

'I don't see why you're making such a fuss about this! It's not like I'm asking you to do anything you haven't done before. Just . . . go through the motions, and put on a good show.'

Leslie looked worried; but not by her. 'What if something comes?'

'Nothing ever has before,' said June.

Leslie looked back at the shadows. It was easier than meeting her eyes.

'I don't know what to believe any more.'

'Stop being such a drama queen,' June said briskly. 'We need something to hold the viewers' attention.'

'We've already given them a murder,' said Leslie.

'Audiences need regular feeding,' said June.

Leslie shrugged resignedly. 'As you wish, oh mistress of the night.'

'Come on,' said June. 'What's the worst that can happen?'

Leslie shook his head. 'I can't believe you said that.'

'Wimp!' said June. She looked round the group, smiled suddenly, and struck a dramatic pose. 'It's *Spooky Time!*'

Leslie glared at her. 'How am I supposed to summon spirits from the vasty deeps, with you polluting the spiritual atmosphere?'

'Would you like us to draw you a pentacle?' Alistair said politely. 'Or send out for a goat, so you can spill its blood and do horrible things with its entrails?'

'What films have you been watching?' said Diana.

'I grew up reading Dennis Wheatley,' said Alistair. 'My father had every horror book that man wrote.'

'Much becomes clear,' said Diana.

Toby glared at them until they stopped talking, and then nodded to Leslie.

'What do you want us to do?'

Leslie gestured at the sleeping bags. 'Sit down, and form a circle. Like we did before, but this time with everyone looking in.'

'What's wrong with sitting on the chairs?' Diana said immediately. 'After a whole evening in heels, my back is killing me.'

'Sitting on the floor will make for a tighter and more secure circle,' Leslie said patiently. 'And you'll all feel more relaxed.'

'Speak for yourself,' said Diana.

'Oh no,' said Leslie. 'There's nothing relaxing about what I'm going to have to do. Sit down, everyone. Get as close to each other as you can. Don't leave room for anything to get in.'

'And just like that, I've gone off the idea,' said Diana.

'Sit,' said Toby.

They pushed the sleeping bags together and sat down on them, shoulder pressed against shoulder. Leslie arranged himself comfortably, looked round the circle, and nodded approvingly.

'Now, everyone hold hands, please. Not too tightly, just a nice firm contact, so you can draw on your neighbour's strength as well as your own.'

Everyone reached out and clasped hands, somewhat self-consciously. Alistair did his best to hide a smile. When they had a demon bearing down on them, they couldn't wait to grab hands; but now they were doing it of their own free will, suddenly no one could meet anyone else's eyes. It felt like adults playing a children's game, without benefit of booze.

June suddenly let go of Alistair's hand, to scratch vigorously at one side of her beehive hairdo.

'What's the matter?' Diana said sweetly. 'Bats in the belfry?'

'You have no idea how uncomfortable this hairdo can get,' June said sourly. 'Normally, I only have to put up with it for an hour. I hadn't realized what a pain it would be, wearing it all night.'

'Then let your hair down,' said Diana. 'You're among friends. Sort of.'

'I can't,' said June. 'It takes ages to put all of this in place, and twice as long to dismantle it. There's interior scaffolding, enough hairspray to blast a new hole in the ozone layer, and any number of hairpins to prevent anything from straying.'

She pulled out one of the long steel pins to show Diana, and then slipped it carefully back into place.

'I never knew fashion could be such a pain,' Alistair said solemnly.

'Men!' June said to Diana. 'They have no idea . . . Besides, this is part of my image, as host of *Spooky Time!* I am the face of this show.'

Toby started to say something, caught June's gaze, and decided not to.

Leslie raised his voice meaningfully. 'If everybody is quite ready, I would like to make a start . . .'

'All right,' said June. 'Don't get out of your pram.'

She grabbed hold of Diana's hand, and held it up so Leslie could see it. The medium nodded approvingly, and then closed his eyes and concentrated on his breathing. Everyone sat very still, so as not to distract him. Time passed. Nothing happened. Diana cleared her throat.

'Aren't you going to start with, "Is there anybody there?" That is traditional, isn't it?'

Leslie didn't answer her. There was nothing in his face to suggest he'd even heard her. The group settled themselves, as patiently as they could manage. After a while, Toby raised his head and looked around him.

'Is it just me, or is it getting darker?'

Everyone stared suspiciously at the shadows pressing in from every side. Alistair quickly raised his voice.

'I made a point of counting all the lights that were still working, and I can assure you that the number hasn't changed. It is not getting any darker.'

'But it feels darker,' Diana said slowly. 'It feels like . . . Walking down a country lane late at night. When there aren't any street lights, and you don't dare look back in case something awful is following you.'

Toby raised an eyebrow. 'What kind of country lanes have you been walking down?'

'There's nothing in the hall with us,' Alistair said firmly. 'I'm not seeing, hearing, or feeling anything out of the ordinary.'

'Only because you're trying so hard not to,' said Diana. 'Have a little faith, Bish.'

'Look at Leslie,' June said quietly.

The medium was sitting slumped forward. His head had dropped so far that his chin was almost resting on his chest. With his eyes closed, he could have been fast asleep.

'Somebody kick him,' said Diana.

'I was thinking about that,' said Toby.

'Better not,' said June. 'That man can sulk like you wouldn't believe.'

'All right,' said Diana. 'Is there a plan? I mean, as and when Leslie actually feels like contributing something . . . Do we send out a general appeal for help, or just hope that someone among the recently departed feels like being helpful, and drops by to give us the good word?'

'Don't look at me,' said June. 'We usually have long talks in advance, before we do anything like this.'

'So Leslie can base his performance on personal information dug up by your researchers?' said Alistair.

'Of course,' said June. She glanced at Leslie, and lowered her voice. 'Actually, he really is very good at this. He always knows exactly what to say, and how far he can go. All he has to do is start the ball rolling in the right direction, and nine times out of ten the guests will fill in the details themselves. You'd be amazed at how quickly people will snap at the flimsiest of bait.'

'But now we're playing it for real,' said Toby. 'I want the truth.'

'Even if it doesn't turn out to be what you thought it would?' said Alistair.

Toby stared at him. 'How do you mean?'

'I've been thinking,' said Alistair. 'What if Indira wasn't

murdered? I mean, we have no proof, no evidence. Nothing
to suggest a motive, let alone a method.'

'Of course it was murder!' said Toby. 'What else could it be?'

'I don't know,' Alistair said reasonably. 'That's the point.
We don't know enough to know anything. We should wait for
the police, and their forensic experts. Just because we couldn't
find a natural cause for Indira's death, doesn't mean there
wasn't one.'

Toby shook his head stubbornly. 'You don't want it to be
murder, because you don't want to believe one of us could be
a killer. But I never doubted it. I just need to know who.'

'And then?' said Alistair.

Toby smiled slowly. It was a cold and very dangerous smile,
and everyone stirred uncomfortably as Toby looked around
the circle.

'When I know who did it,' he said, 'I'll make them pay.'

Alistair looked steadily at Toby. 'Any man who sets out to
seek vengeance should dig two graves.'

Toby turned his unsettling smile on Alistair. 'I can live with
that.'

And then they all looked round sharply as Leslie's head
came up. His face was completely lacking in emotion, but
there was a new sense of purpose about him. Suddenly, he
looked like a man who knew what he was doing. Alistair
glanced down as Diana's hand tightened on his, and then he
looked quickly round the group. He could feel a new tension
coursing through the circle of closed hands, like the current
from some unknown power source. Leslie started talking, his
words slow and blurred, as though he was dreaming.

'Is there anyone present who wishes to speak? All are
welcome here. Step forward, my friends, and make yourself
known. We are here to hear you.'

June grinned at Alistair. 'He always starts with that. I wrote
it for him.'

'Somehow, I'm not in the least surprised,' said Diana.

'Hush!' Toby said harshly. 'We're finally getting
somewhere.'

Leslie's head swivelled slowly back and forth, and though
his eyes remained closed, he seemed to be searching the

surrounding shadows. The others took a quick look too, but couldn't see anything. Diana scowled at the medium, and stirred unhappily.

'I swear, if he says, "Has anyone here lost a loved one whose name begins with R", I will slap the life out of him.'

And then she made a sharp pained sound, as Toby's hand clamped down hard on hers. She glowered at him, but took the hint and stopped talking. The medium was sitting very still, all his concentration focused on something only he could hear. And then everyone jumped, as he suddenly started talking again.

'So many shapes, gathering in the gloom. Visitors, from the long night. Ghosts, from times long gone. Crowding around us, pressing forward. I never saw so many revenants in one place . . .'

Diana looked at June. 'Did you write that as well?'

'Oh please,' said June. 'I'd never go for anything that obvious. He's ad-libbing.'

Toby glared at June and she glared right back at him. And then everyone looked at Leslie, as he addressed the circle with a new urgency in his voice.

'Tell me what to ask! There are things that have come a long way to be here, and I don't know how long they'll stay. Hurry! Don't leave me exposed in the long night, alone and unprotected. I can feel greater presences starting to take an interest in us.'

Alistair leaned forward. 'What kind of presences?'

'For every kind of prey, there is a predator,' said Leslie. 'Ask your questions!'

'I need to speak to Indira,' said Toby.

'She isn't here,' said Leslie.

Toby glared at him. 'Of course she's here! She's in the kitchen!'

'That isn't her,' said Leslie. 'That's what she left behind. Indira has moved on, to the place prepared for her. But Gregory is here.'

Toby made a startled sound, as much shock as surprise.

'You know that name,' said Alistair.

'Of course I know it,' said Toby. 'It's my friend. The one who died, and appeared to me in a mirror.'

He looked at Leslie for a long moment, as though unsure whether he wanted to continue. But then he braced himself and raised his voice, addressing the shadows as much as the medium.

'Gregory? This is Toby. Can you hear me?'

A new voice issued from Leslie's mouth, though the medium's expression never changed.

'Toby, boy. It's been a while, hasn't it? What are you doing in this terrible place? After I went to so much trouble to warn you . . .'

'Is that what that was?' said Toby. 'Why didn't you say something?'

'It's not easy, boy, making your way back across the grey marshes. Past all the guardians, and the liers-in-wait. You shouldn't be here, boy. You have wandered off the path, and the beasts of the outer dark have your scent.'

'I'm not here for myself,' said Toby. 'I need to know who killed Indira.'

'She's beyond your help. And that's all I have to say, Toby boy. Except: be seeing you.'

The voice in Leslie's mouth laughed softly, and the sound seemed to just fade away, as though receding into the distance. Toby called after his friend, but there was no response. Toby slowly sat back again, looking distinctly unsettled.

'That wasn't what you'd hoped for, was it?' Diana said kindly.

'What do you have to do to get a straight answer round here?' said Toby.

'Did that voice really sound like your friend?' said Alistair.

'It was Gregory,' said Toby. 'I'd know him anywhere.'

Alistair shot a glance at June and Leslie, and then leaned over so he could murmur in Toby's ear.

'June already admitted she and Leslie research their guests before they run a séance.'

Toby shook his head stubbornly. 'I know my friends' voices when I hear them.' He turned away to scowl at Leslie. 'Why can't you make contact with Indira?'

'He already told you why not,' said June. 'She's gone.'

Toby ignored her to glare at Leslie. 'There must be something more you can do!'

Alistair cleared his throat loudly. 'You really shouldn't take all of this so seriously, Toby. Never trust a medium, especially when they've got an audience to impress.'

And then he broke off as Leslie's back arched, and his whole body tensed. Alistair and June both winced as the medium's hands crushed theirs. Leslie's face twisted, and he let out a heart-rending moan. June waited until she was sure he had finished, and then leaned forward.

'Try to remember you're a professional! There's no need to take it that far over the top.'

Leslie slowly lowered his head, and one by one his straining muscles relaxed. He frowned around him with his eyes closed, as though puzzled.

'So many presences . . . But I didn't summon them.'

'Then who did?' Alistair said politely.

'You did,' said Leslie. 'All of you. These are your ghosts, from your pasts.'

June shuddered suddenly. 'Is it me, or did it just get cold?'

'Yes!' said Diana. 'It does feel cold.'

'Really cold,' said Toby.

Alistair was surprised to find he felt cold too. He looked quickly round the circle, but there was no breath steaming from anyone's mouth. The phrase 'group hysteria' moved quickly through his mind, but he didn't say anything. He kept his gaze fixed on Leslie, intrigued to see where the medium would take the séance next.

'So many interested parties,' Leslie said slowly. 'So many things left unsaid. So many secrets that were never shared, only left to fester. So easy to let the moment pass, because we always think there'll be more time, until suddenly there isn't. And then it's too late for ever.' He nodded slowly. 'Ask your questions. They're all here, but they won't stay long. Not in a place like this.'

Everyone looked at everyone else. The séance had taken a turn none of them had expected. Leslie's voice cracked like a whip.

'Ask your questions! Before something bad comes sniffing round from the outer rings!'

'OK,' said Diana. 'I'll bite the bullet.' She put on her best stage voice, to make sure it would travel to all parts of the hall. 'This is Diana Hunt. If you have something to say to me, get on with it. Otherwise, leave a message with my agent.'

Leslie didn't turn his head in her direction, but suddenly a young woman's voice issued from his mouth, high and breathy.

'Diana . . . How could you leave me behind?'

Diana's face was suddenly full of shock and horror. It was clear she recognized the new voice. She tried to say something, but stumbled over the words.

'We had such hopes, such dreams . . .' the young woman said through Leslie. 'All the amazing things we were going to do. How could you grab the gold ring, but kick me into the gutter? We made a vow that whoever got the first big break would take the other with them.' The voice was suddenly sharper, harsher. 'What's the matter, Diana? Cat got your tongue?'

Leslie stopped talking. The silence dragged on, until Diana had to say something. She swallowed hard, and forced the words out.

'Mary? Is that you, Mary?'

'It was all your fault,' said the voice. 'None of it would have happened if you'd just kept your word.'

'They didn't want you,' said Diana. Her stage voice was gone, replaced by something smaller. 'I did try to pressure them into finding a part for you, but they just said, "You're in no position to make demands. Stop being a pain, or we'll find someone else." I couldn't risk losing the part!'

'You should have tried harder,' said the voice.

Diana started to answer, and then stopped herself. She took a deep breath, and when she spoke again she was back in control.

'I had to make a hard choice, Mary. Because that's what professionals do. You told me you understood.'

'Oh I did,' said Mary. 'I understood I could never be a star, because I wasn't strong like you. It cuts deep, when you realize you aren't worthy of your dreams. So I did what I had to do. I just didn't realize how many pills it would take . . .'

Leslie stopped talking. Diana sat hunched over, as though wrapped around some inner pain.

'Did she kill herself?' Alistair said quietly.

'No,' said Diana. 'She didn't take enough pills. She survived, but with major brain damage. Spent her last few years mumbling to herself in a sanitorium. Until a nurse left her alone in the bath, and she just slipped under the water and drowned. I didn't even hear about it until years later.'

'It wasn't your fault,' said Alistair. 'We're all responsible for our own lives, and our own choices.'

Diana leaned in close beside him. 'How could Leslie know all that? I never told anyone!'

'Mediums often have paid sources, in hospitals and the like,' Alistair said carefully.

'But that was Mary's voice!' Diana said angrily. 'I'd know it anywhere!'

'Would you?' said Alistair. 'After all this time?'

Diana turned back to Leslie. 'Mary? Are you still there?'

'She has nothing more to say,' said Leslie.

'But I need to talk to her . . .'

'She doesn't want to know.'

Alistair muttered urgently to Diana. 'Don't let him get to you. You don't have to believe any of this.'

'Yes I do,' said Diana. 'It's my penance. You should know all about that.' She flashed him a brittle, angry smile, and turned to Leslie. 'It's the bishop's turn. Who has dropped by to accuse him?'

Leslie started to speak again, his eyes firmly closed and his face empty of any expression. This time the voice was that of a middle-aged woman, heavy with hoarded anger.

'It was your decision, Alistair. You knew what it would do to your dad, but you did it anyway. We sacrificed everything, so you could have the kind of life we never did. We were so proud, the day you went off to university. The first in our family ever to do that. But it was always understood, everything we did for you was so you could get a proper job, and make good money, and look after us. You had such a future . . . And you threw it all away! Broke your dad's heart . . .'

Leslie stopped talking. Alistair just stared at him. After a while, the voice in Leslie's mouth started speaking again. 'I don't know where you got all that religious nonsense from. Certainly not from us. We always had more sense. You could have been someone big; your dad and me would never have had to worry again. But no . . . You turned your back on us to join the church! To help other people, you said. But what about your dad and me?'

Alistair sat very still, his face set in harsh lines. Diana watched him for a while, and all the anger went out of her. Because the pain in her recognized the pain in him.

'Was that your mother's voice?' she said quietly.

'It sounded like her,' said Alistair. His voice was perfectly steady. 'And it was the kind of thing she used to say. God knows I heard it often enough. But that wasn't her.'

'How can you be so sure?' said Diana. 'Oh, wait a minute; is she still alive?'

'No,' said Alistair. 'She died years ago, spitting her disappointment at me right to the end. And with her gone, my father just faded away. I do my best to believe they're happy together, in a better place. Because that's my job.'

'Are you OK, Alistair?' said Diana. She tried to keep the worry out of her voice, even though she could see past the cold expression on his face to the anger underneath. Aimed not at his parents, but at the man who claimed to speak for them. 'Is there anything you want to say . . .?'

Alistair thought for a moment, and then his face relaxed. 'It is a shame they never got to see me be a television star. I think they would have liked that.'

'You could tell them now,' said Toby.

'That wasn't my mother,' said Alistair. He stared coldly round the circle. 'This is what mediums do, what they live for. The chance to press people's buttons, and take advantage of their vulnerabilities. Make people feel so bad they'll do anything, pay anything, so the medium will make contact with their loved ones and put things right. They prey on our guilt, on our sins of omission.'

'On what?' said Diana.

'All the things we know we should have done, but didn't,'

said Alistair. 'Perhaps the hardest of sins to forgive ourselves for.'

He looked at Leslie, and let the anger drop out of his face and his voice.

'I made peace with my parents long ago. I had to forgive myself, so I could teach others how to do it. You pushed all the wrong buttons, Leslie. You didn't get to me at all.'

Diana wasn't so sure about that.

Alistair turned abruptly to face June. 'Well, that's it. Game over. Unless there's any more nasty tricks you want your pet medium to play?' He waited for June to say something, and when she didn't Alistair turned to Toby. 'Well, you've had your séance. Was it everything you hoped it would be?'

Toby scowled at Leslie. 'I didn't get to talk to Indira. And I'm still no nearer understanding what happened.'

'Of course not,' said Alistair. 'He was never going to give you any answers, because he never had any. He's just another con man, with a good act and a gift for mimicry.' His voice lashed out one last time. 'Call it a day, Leslie. It's over.'

The medium stirred slowly. His face was still calm, his eyes still closed. The bishop's angry words seemed to have washed right over him, and not touched him at all. When he spoke, it was in his own voice.

'It's not over yet.'

'Why not?' said Diana. 'You've had a go at everyone.'

'Not everyone,' said Leslie. And slowly, he turned his closed eyes in June's direction. She sat up straight and glared at him.

'You wouldn't dare . . .'

Leslie nodded easily at the shadows, as though inviting a host of unseen presences to bear witness.

'I didn't call any of these people here. They came of their own free will, because they had things they wanted to say.'

June faced him squarely. 'And what is it you think you've dug up on me, you little weasel? Do you really think you've got some dirt to spill? You should know better than to go head to head with me. After all the interviews I've given, all the chat shows I've been on, the autobiography I had ghost-written that I really should get around to reading one of these days . . . I told everyone everything!'

I have no secrets! That's why my audience loves me; because they think they know me.'

She glared quickly around the circle, being angry at them before they could be angry at her.

'You have to be hard on everyone, including yourself, if you're going to get on in this business. And no one's harder on me than me.' She turned her gaze back to Leslie. 'There's no one for you to channel, nothing you can say that I couldn't bear to hear. If all the people I've ever done wrong were standing right here in front of me, I'd laugh in their faces. Because they made me what I am. So go on, Leslie. Give it your best shot. Who is it that's turned up, to pluck at my heart-strings?'

'No one,' said Leslie.

June looked at him blankly. 'What?'

'No one,' said Leslie. 'No one came to talk to you, because nobody cares.'

June seemed to crumple in on herself for a moment, but when she straightened up again her face was perfectly composed.

'I never needed anyone. Least of all you, you treacherous little snake. Now snap out of that trance. We've thrown enough raw meat to our viewers. It's time to move on, and find something else to hold their attention.'

She deliberately jerked her hands out of Diana and Leslie's grasp, breaking the circle. She leaned in close to Toby, shoving her face right into his.

'Well? Did you get your money's worth?'

She turned away without waiting for an answer. Everyone in the group let go of everyone's hands, and they all relaxed a little. The tense atmosphere of the séance had completely disappeared. June growled at Leslie.

'Come on, snap out of it. There's work to be done.'

Leslie drew in a deep, shuddering breath, and slowly shook his head. When he opened his eyes, he was immediately his old self again.

'Well now, did anything interesting happen while I was out?'

'I ought to punch you in the head,' said Diana.

Leslie smiled. 'That good, eh? I hope someone was taking notes.'

'You didn't tell us anything we needed to know,' said Diana.

'Nothing about Indira,' said Alistair.

'And nothing at all about the weird shit that keeps happening,' said Diana. 'You just raked up a few bad decisions from our past, so you could throw them in our faces.'

'How are you going to come to terms with your past,' Leslie said patiently, 'if you don't face up to it? I'm not in charge during a séance, I just open a door. Who comes through is up to you.' He shook his head sadly. 'People say they want the truth but they don't, not really. All they want are simple platitudes, wrapped in comforting lies, and I was never very good at that. Or I'd still be filling theatres, instead of guest-hosting on a show like this.' He turned to Toby. 'What about you? Nothing to say? Did I get under your skin, and make it crawl?'

They all looked at Toby. He was sitting very still, his head bowed. Alistair gave his shoulder a good shake, and Toby fell over backwards. Diana made a startled sound, and scrambled up on to her feet. June and Leslie did the same, and moved hurriedly to stand together. Alistair knelt beside Toby and checked quickly for vital signs, but there weren't any. He turned to the others.

'I'm sorry. There's nothing I can do. He's dead.'

'Can't you try CPR?' said Diana. She stared in horror at the dead man, one hand at her mouth.

'I'm pretty sure he's beyond that,' said Alistair. 'But feel free to try, if you know how.'

'I don't,' said Diana. 'There was a course . . . but I never paid attention.'

Alistair looked at June and Leslie, but they shook their heads. Alistair knew how, but he didn't try. He'd already spotted a small drop of blood on Toby's shirt, right over the heart. Confirming that Toby had been murdered, just like Indira.

June turned suddenly to Leslie. '*What did you do?*'

'It wasn't me!' he protested. 'This is nothing to do with me!'

'Could it have been Toby's heart?' Diana said tentatively.

Alistair shook his head. 'I think we would have noticed the symptoms of a major heart attack.'

'He can't just have died!' said Diana.

Alistair sat back on his haunches, and looked thoughtfully at Toby. He didn't say anything about the blood spot. He was still trying to figure out who he could trust.

'What killed him?' said Diana.

'I'm not seeing any signs of violence,' Alistair said carefully.

'Just like Indira,' said June.

Alistair got to his feet. 'Two sudden and unexplained deaths, without any warning? That can't be coincidence.'

'Maybe while we were all concentrating on each other,' Leslie said slowly, 'someone sneaked in from the shadows and killed him.'

'Without any of us noticing?' said Diana.

'There were powers present . . .' said Leslie.

Diana rounded on him furiously. 'Don't start that again!' She glared Leslie into silence, and then turned to Alistair. 'Could his death have been stress-related? From the séance, and the revelations?'

'Again, I think we would have noticed that level of stress,' said Alistair. He looked steadily at the surviving members of the group. 'We need to move him somewhere safe and secure. Preserve any trace evidence the killer might have left on the body.'

'We could put him in the kitchen, with Indira,' said Diana.

'Yes,' said Alistair. 'He'd like that. They can keep each other company.'

He knelt down and carefully rolled Toby on to a single sleeping bag. Then he organized everyone else into picking up the bag, and together they carried Toby into the kitchen.

They crammed Toby in beside Indira, on top of the ovens. It took some effort to get him to stay put, and by the time they'd finished, everyone was out of breath. The moment Toby was securely in place, June and Leslie hurried out of the kitchen. Alistair stood before the body and quietly said his prayer for the dead; this time Diana stayed with him, head bowed. When Alistair was done, he smiled briefly at Diana.

'Getting religious?'

'There are no atheists on the killing ground,' said Diana. 'And we definitely have a killer in our midst.'

'The number of suspects is shrinking,' said Alistair.

'I can't believe it's you, and I know it isn't me,' said Diana. 'That just leaves June, and Leslie.'

'So it would seem,' said Alistair.

Diana looked at him narrowly. 'Are you saying you see me as a suspect?'

'I'm trying very hard not to,' said Alistair.

Diana sniffed loudly. 'Why would June or Leslie want to sabotage their own comeback show, by killing off their guests?'

'They know the camera positions better than anyone,' Alistair said reasonably. 'They could have worked out in advance how to kill someone and not be noticed.'

'But we were all sitting in a circle!' said Diana. 'Holding hands! Neither of them could have attacked Toby without one of us noticing. But . . . who else is there?'

'That's the point, isn't it?' said Alistair. 'We've already established that the hall is completely empty, apart from us, and locked up tight.'

Diana faced Alistair squarely. 'I'm no more a killer than you are.'

'But how well do we really know each other?' said Alistair.

Diana smiled briefly. 'After listening to Leslie and his voices, I'd have to say a little better than we did before.'

'I'm wondering if there might have been a motive tucked away somewhere in those accusations,' said Alistair.

'But everyone in those stories was dead,' said Diana. 'That was the point.'

'Victims can have friends,' said Alistair. 'And avenging angels. Unless you think a ghost killed Toby?'

Diana sniffed. 'Seems unlikely. Do you think the killer is done with his work?'

'We don't know why these people died,' said Alistair. 'So that makes it hard to predict any future actions.'

Diana scowled. 'Really wasn't what I wanted to hear.'

'That's how you know something is probably true,' said Alistair.

'Let's get out of here,' said Diana. 'This room is giving me the creeps.'

'But this is the one place we can be sure we're safe,' said Alistair. 'Because everyone else in the room is dead.'

Diana shook her head firmly. 'Really not helping, Bish.'

Alistair led her over to the kitchen door, and went to turn the light off. Diana put a hand on his arm.

'I don't like to think of them lying here, in the dark.'

Alistair left the light on, and quietly closed the kitchen door.

Out in the foyer, Diana paused to study Alistair carefully.

'Did any of that stuff in the séance get to you? Leslie was throwing it pretty hard.'

Alistair shook his head. 'Once I recognized what he was doing, it was just water off a bishop's back.'

'Do you think there were any actual ghosts present?'

'No,' said Alistair. 'Leslie was careful to keep his accusations vague. Presented in the most emotional terms, of course, so he could get a good rise out of us. But everything we heard could have been uncovered by any reasonably determined researcher.'

'But we all recognized the voices,' said Diana.

'Did we?' said Alistair. 'Imitating other people has always been a standard weapon in a medium's repertoire. The voices probably weren't that close; we just assumed they were, in the heat of the moment.'

Diana nodded slowly. 'Didn't you find anything of interest on Toby's body?'

Alistair hesitated, and then decided it was time for a leap of faith.

'I have to trust someone,' he said. 'And I choose you.'

He quickly filled her in on the small spot of blood he'd found on Toby and Indira's clothes.

Diana frowned. 'Maybe the killer is marking their victims?'

'You mean some kind of message?' said Alistair. 'If it is, it's going right over my head.'

Diana smiled suddenly. 'What matters is: you trust me and

I trust you. Which means either June or Leslie has to be the murderer! That simplifies things.'

'So far, nothing has been simple,' said Alistair.

They went back into the main hall, to find June and Leslie caught up in a heated argument and glaring into each other's faces. They broke off immediately the side door opened, and by the time Alistair and Diana had joined them, the two hosts were back in control of themselves.

'You've been gone a long time,' June said accusingly.

'We were showing respect for the dead,' said Diana. 'What were you two arguing about?'

'The usual,' said Leslie. 'Why is all this bad stuff happening, and what can we do about it?'

'There's only one thing we can do,' said Diana. 'Get the hell out of here.'

'There is no way out!' said June. 'We've already been through this.'

'Indira and Toby found a way out,' said Alistair.

Leslie glared at him. 'I don't think that's funny.'

'Toby would have laughed,' said Alistair.

Diana looked at Leslie. 'You were able to channel Indira, for a while. Could you call Toby back, to talk about his murder?'

'I'm tired,' said Leslie. 'Worn out. I couldn't raise a smile, let alone the recently departed.'

'If we don't work out what's going on here soon,' said Alistair, 'we'll be able to ask Toby and Indira in person who killed them.'

EIGHT

The Truth, by All Means

June and Leslie stood shoulder to shoulder, the better to glare at Alistair, who just stood his ground and stared calmly back at them. Diana moved in beside Alistair, and turned her own glare on Leslie and June. Alistair could feel the tension building, and knew it wouldn't be long before somebody said something they might regret. Which meant it was down to him to try and ease the situation. In his experience, the best way to do that was to persuade someone to offer an apology that both sides knew wasn't in the least sincere, but would allow everyone to step back from the brink while still saving some face. But even as Alistair started to say something, June cut in and spoke right over him.

'You're always so quick to criticize, but I don't see you doing anything useful to help!'

Alistair was taken aback by the sheer vehemence in her voice, but as he struggled to frame a suitable response, Diana jumped in to defend him, her eyes blazing just as fiercely as June's.

'You mean except for when he stood up to save us all from that demon? You do remember that, don't you?'

It was June's turn to be taken aback. She wasn't used to being challenged so directly. But she didn't so much as glance at Leslie for support, and ignored Diana so she could concentrate her attack on Alistair.

'We don't know that there is a murderer! We don't understand anything that's going on in this place! All we can be sure of is that none of us will survive to see the morning if we allow ourselves to be distracted by a murder mystery that probably isn't even real!'

Alistair put on his best *I'm going to be calm and reasonable about this because somebody has to be and clearly it isn't going to be you* tone of voice.

'I thought you and Leslie were supposed to be the experts, when it came to supernatural events and out-of-this-world phenomena? That is what it says on your publicity handouts.'

'Those two?' said Diana. 'They're not experts; they just play them on television.' She concentrated her glare on Leslie, as the weaker of the two hosts. 'You told us you'd never experienced any real spooky stuff on any of your shows, until tonight.'

Leslie looked apologetically at June. 'I did say that, because technically it's not entirely untrue.' He switched his gaze to Alistair. 'Events are getting out of control. We have to do something to protect ourselves.'

'I know something we can do,' said Diana.

Everyone looked at her, and Diana bristled as she took in the sceptical expressions on display before her.

'There was no need for all of you to look so utterly amazed. I am capable of the occasional flash of brilliance.'

'Wouldn't doubt it for a moment,' Alistair said quickly. 'What did you have in mind?'

Diana smiled at him dazzlingly, and then nodded to Leslie. 'We use his psychic abilities to get in direct touch with whoever or whatever is behind all these supernatural attacks. We're not just facing a bunch of unrelated weirdness; there has to be an operating force driving everything, from behind the scenes.'

'Actually,' said Alistair, 'that is a very good idea.'

Diana looked at him coldly. 'That would have made a much better compliment without the clear note of surprise in your voice.'

'I'm just surprised at your choice of potential saviour,' Alistair said smoothly. 'Do you honestly believe that man is the real thing?'

Diana thought about it. Leslie raised an eyebrow, in a hurt sort of way.

'The jury is still out,' Diana said finally. 'But, we have to work with what we've got.'

June produced a brief smile, with little or no real humour in it.

'Leslie has worked on my show for years, and I have yet to see him do anything that would even remotely qualify as psychic. Head games, con games, and funny voices are more in his line. All of which have proved very useful, at various times.'

'Thank you,' Leslie said dryly. 'I like to think I provide a useful function.'

'Don't push your luck,' said June, not even glancing at him.

Alistair considered June thoughtfully. 'You were quick enough to support his séance. At least one part of which seemed to hit you where you lived.'

June met his gaze unflinchingly. 'When the boat is sinking, you grab at anything that might float.'

'I think I've just been insulted,' said Leslie.

'If you're not certain, I need to put more effort into it,' said June.

Diana rose above their never-ending squabbling, so she could concentrate a determined stare on Leslie.

'You've done some impressive things tonight. Have faith in yourself, and your abilities, because we need you to find out what's behind everything that's been thrown at us. Not just the weird shit, but the murders as well.' She broke off, to look quickly at Alistair and June. 'Does anyone here still believe Indira and Toby died from natural causes? No, didn't think so . . . moving on. Let's start with: why did the supernatural events only start happening when we moved into the hall?'

'Don't you put the blame on my show!' said June.

'It did occur to me,' Leslie said slowly, 'that when we moved in and started making changes to the structure of the hall, we might have woken up something.'

'Hush, Leslie,' June said briskly. 'Grown-ups talking.'

Leslie rounded on her, like a dog that has been teased once too often.

'There's more going on here than meets your eye! If you can't bring yourself to accept the otherworldly nature of what we're facing, the odds are we'll all be dead before the locks open!'

June looked at him, and for once didn't immediately move to slap him down.

'Say you did disturb something,' said Diana. 'And it woke up angry. If that is the case, then we need to figure out how to put it back to sleep again. If I have to believe in Leslie the Mighty Psychic to do that . . . Well, I've believed stranger things in my time. I am an actress, after all.'

Alistair looked steadily at Leslie. 'What do you think? Are you ready to step up, and be the man who saves the day?'

Leslie looked down at his hands, clasped tightly together before him, as though nerving himself to do something he wasn't sure he was capable of. Which struck Alistair as interesting: Leslie hadn't shown any doubt in his abilities before. In fact, he'd always been quite enthusiastic about showing them off. Leslie finally raised his head, and looked at June.

'This isn't what I do. You know that.'

June sniffed. 'On my show, you do whatever I tell you to.'

Leslie flared up again. 'This was never your show! It's our show! I own twenty-five per cent; that was in my contract, right from the beginning!'

June locked eyes with him, not giving an inch to the medium's sudden show of defiance.

'All right; you own a percentage of my show. I'm still the one in charge, the one who makes all the decisions and gets things done.'

'What would you do if I decided to sell my percentage?' said Leslie. 'And you had to deal with a new partner who wouldn't let you walk all over him? You'd be in real trouble then!'

June hit him with her most professional smile. 'I know how to handle junior partners. And I can always get a new pet medium. The woods are full of them.'

Leslie looked honestly outraged. 'You'd drop me, just like that? After everything I've brought to this show?'

'You're either with me or against me,' said June. 'And you've seen the things I'm prepared to do, to deal with people who aren't on my side.'

Leslie nodded slowly, as all the fight went out of him.

'You really want me to do this?'

'We have to do something,' said June. She gestured at the

wall cameras. 'The audience are waiting for us to pull a dramatic rabbit out of the hat. You doing your "mysterious powers of the mind" bit could be just what we need to get the audience back on our side. On what has to be the most shambolic show I've ever been involved with.'

'But one of the most dramatic,' said Alistair.

Diana looked at him. 'You say that like it's a good thing.'

Alistair smiled at her. 'Be honest: aren't you enjoying yourself, just a bit?'

'Well,' said Diana, 'maybe, just a little. In between the moments of stark terror.'

'It's all providing food for thought,' said Alistair.

Diana shook her head. 'There are times when I have no idea what's going on in your head.'

'Probably just as well, sometimes,' said Alistair. 'Ever since I met you, not all my thoughts have been fit for family viewing.'

'Easy, Bish,' said Diana. 'Not in front of the audience.'

'When you two have quite finished throwing handfuls of hormones at each other,' June said coldly, 'we still have work to do. If there's even a chance Leslie can calm things down, we have to go for it.' She nodded to him. 'Give me maximum medium: you're on.'

Leslie adopted his most professional air. 'What do you want me to do?'

'The usual, only bigger,' said June. 'Make some noise, attract something's attention, and then pour psychic oil on the troubled waters. Get the ear of whoever's in charge around here.'

'I thought that was you,' said Leslie.

'Very droll,' said June. 'Now stop putting it off and get us some answers.'

Leslie looked at the shadows surrounding them, as though trying to judge the strength of an opponent.

'There's more to this place than we thought,' he said slowly. 'A lot of things have been happening that we didn't allow for.'

'But we're still running this show,' said June.

The two of them stared at each other, and Alistair was sure he saw something pass between them.

'Just reach out,' June said finally. 'See if something will talk through you. The audience always loves it when you do that.'

Leslie brightened at the thought. 'They do, don't they? You can always rely on me to hold the audience's attention.'

Some of his confidence returned, now that he was back on familiar ground. Thinking only in terms of what was best for the show, and how good he'd look doing it. He didn't quite wink at June, but he did draw himself up and stand a little straighter.

'Time to wow the crowds and dazzle them with footwork. Hit them so hard they never see it coming; and make them love us for it.'

'Go for it,' said June.

'No!' said Diana. 'You can't get away with just going through the motions; not this time! We need solid information about what's behind all of this.'

'I'm not sure you've chosen the right person for the job,' Alistair murmured.

Diana rounded on him. 'You were all for it, just a minute ago! Or are you suggesting we put our faith in God, and hope he comes through with a miracle?'

'It's a better idea than putting your faith in someone else's pet medium,' said Alistair.

'You have no idea what I'm capable of,' said Leslie.

He looked ready to say a whole lot more, but June grabbed him by the shoulders and marched him over to the piled-up sleeping bags in the middle of the room. Then she looked quickly at the cameras, to make sure they'd get good coverage of the medium as he got ready to spring into psychic action. She clapped Leslie briskly on the shoulder, as though encouraging a dog to show off its one good trick, before moving back to stand with Alistair and Diana.

'Right!' she said to Leslie. 'You're on! Reach out to the infinite, and don't take no for an answer.'

Leslie closed his eyes, breathed deeply, and put on his best medium's voice, rich and resonant enough to reach all four corners of the hall.

'Whoever is here, please make yourself known to us. It's

important that we understand what is happening in this place.'

All the overhead tube lights suddenly snapped back on, filling the hall with a dazzling glare. Everyone cried out, and raised an arm to shield their eyes. They'd been stuck in the gloom for so long they were half-blinded by the intense light. They'd barely recovered from that when vast deafening sounds blasted at them from every direction at once. Massive rolls of thunder, followed by great and terrible voices, speaking in unknown languages. Wild and fierce, loud beyond bearing. Alistair thought they sounded like alien gods, come down to Earth in a really bad mood. Then the voices were drowned out by savage howls and shrieks, like predators on the prowl, in search of victims.

The sheer pandemonium battered away at everyone in what felt like a determined assault, hitting them from every side at once. Alistair and Diana huddled together for mutual support. Alistair took out the crucifix he wore round his neck and held it high, to no obvious effect, while Diana glared around her, ready to lash out at anything that got too close. June looked more angry than scared, ready to defy anything that dared threaten her show. Leslie raised his voice, struggling to make himself heard above the bedlam.

'Calm yourself! There's no need for any of this. It's important that we work together . . .'

The sounds and the voices cut off abruptly, as though someone had thrown a switch. It was suddenly very quiet in the hall, and very still; like the peace after a storm has passed. One by one the overhead tube lights began to flicker and go out, until all that remained were the few that had been lit before. The shadows returned, deeper and darker than ever. Alistair put away his crucifix, and Diana threw her arms around him.

'You were really brave, darling!'

'So were you,' said Alistair. He waited a moment. 'You can let go of me now.'

She hugged him a little tighter. 'Are you sure that's what you want?'

'There is a time and a place,' said Alistair.

'Looking forward to it, darling.'

They shared a brief smile, and stepped away from each other.

Leslie stood slumped and exhausted, but still managed to look pleased with himself. June rushed over and hugged him fiercely. Just for a moment, and then she fell back a step, still smiling right into his face. Leslie looked surprised, and then just a little shocked, at such an unexpected display of emotion.

'That was more like it!' said June. 'High point of the show! Do you have any idea as to what just happened?'

'Not really,' said Leslie. 'I just went with the flow. But then, you never did appreciate what I'm capable of.'

He broke off, a look of complete surprise filling his face. He tried to say something to June, and then all the strength went out of his legs and he collapsed. June let out a startled cry, and stumbled backwards. Diana moved quickly over to join her, while Alistair hurried forward to kneel beside Leslie as he lay motionless on the floor. Alistair checked for vital signs, but already knew he wasn't going to find any. He turned to face Diana and June.

'I'm sorry. He's gone.'

'But . . . He can't be dead!' said June. 'He's been with me for so long . . .'

She didn't cry. Alistair was pretty sure June didn't do crying. But her face was suddenly tired, and drawn. Diana put a comforting arm across June's shoulders, but June just stared at Leslie's unmoving body, as though she thought she could will him back to life. Alistair took a moment to close Leslie's staring eyes, and then examined the body carefully.

'No obvious cause of death,' he said. 'Just like the others.'

'There was nobody near us!' said June. 'I would have seen them.'

Alistair found a small spot of blood on Leslie's shirt, directly over the heart; just as he'd expected. He sighed regretfully. He knew what he had to do, but he really wasn't looking forward to it. He rose to his feet and stared steadily at June. Her face was full of pain, regret, and loss. And Alistair didn't believe any of it.

'This last death was my fault,' said Alistair. 'If I'd worked this out sooner, I might have been able to save Leslie; but I really couldn't believe you'd go so far as to kill your own accomplice.'

June stared at him. 'What are you talking about?'

'Good performance, June,' said Alistair. 'But I'm not buying it.'

Diana looked at Alistair, and then at June. She took her arm off June's shoulder, and fell back a step. June didn't even seem to notice, she was staring so hard at Alistair. Diana looked from one to the other, completely thrown by the sudden turn of events.

'Alistair?' she said carefully. 'What's going on?'

'I finally worked out who's behind everything,' said Alistair. 'All the supposedly weird events, and three very real murders. There was nothing supernatural about anything that's happened; it was all smoke and mirrors, and carefully staged tricks. Scripted in advance, by one cold-hearted woman ready to do anything to keep her show going.'

'Have you lost your mind?' said June. She sounded more curious than anything else. She also seemed to have forgotten all about her grief over Leslie's death.

'You tried running reality as though it was a reality show,' said Alistair. 'But the harder you tried, the less real it seemed.'

'You mean everything that's happened here was down to her, all along?' said Diana.

'June was the show's producer, as well as its host,' said Alistair. 'Which meant she was always in control of everything. And determined to put on a comeback show no one would ever forget. Full of fake ghosts, and real dead people, all to save her precious career.'

He paused for a moment, to give June a chance to defend herself, but she had nothing to say. Alistair sighed, and gestured around him at the empty hall.

'You finally overreached yourself with all that noise. It was too carefully orchestrated to be believed. You worked too hard to make sure every part of it could be heard clearly, with no overlapping; and that just doesn't happen in real life.' He nodded to Diana. 'It all came from loudspeakers hidden inside the walls, placed there in advance by June and Leslie. The same loudspeakers produced the fake footsteps, and the knocking sounds. They never echoed because they were created in a studio. Once I worked that out, it was my first clue as to what was really going on.'

'Good for you,' said Diana. 'Now would you mind explaining it, for the slower thinkers in class? What did the fake supernatural stuff have to do with killing people?'

'Do you want to take that, June?' said Alistair. 'Or shall I just keep going?'

June stood very still, her gaze fixed on Alistair. And he kept his eyes fixed on her as he talked to Diana; because a cornered animal is always the most dangerous.

'June set all of this up in advance,' he said. 'Starting with turning off most of the lights, to create a proper atmosphere for the show. We were far more likely to believe in supernatural outbreaks if they took place in a suitably spooky setting. The ghostly sounds were designed to keep us off balance, and provide a sense of danger. I'm guessing they were either triggered by pre-programmed timers, or June had a remote control hidden about her person. I did see her and Leslie comparing watches to check the time, just before the loud knockings began.'

Diana moved in close beside Alistair. 'You're saying June killed Leslie, as well as Indira and Toby? Why would she do that?'

'Let's start with Leslie,' said Alistair. 'Going by the last expression on his face, I don't think it ever occurred to him that he might be in any danger from June. He thought he was safe. Not because of any warm feelings on June's part, but because he was such a vital part of the show they were both working so hard to save. Only it turned out he wasn't that important, after all. What was the last straw, June? Were you worried he wouldn't be able to keep his mouth shut? Or did you decide he had to go when he threatened to sell his percentage of the show, just when you were on track to make it a success again. You couldn't allow him to sabotage your success. Not after you'd gone to so much trouble . . .'

'Damn, June,' said Diana. 'That is seriously cold. Even for show business.'

'Everything we've been through was just a series of manufactured scares,' said Alistair. 'Designed to hit us with one jolt after another, and keep the audience watching. And get the show renewed, of course. I'm guessing June and Leslie already tried out smaller tricks on previous shows, and when they realized what they could get away with . . . they started thinking big. But to create a show that would shock and horrify their somewhat jaded audience, they needed something really dramatic.'

Alistair took a moment to steady himself. It was proving harder than he'd expected, talking to June's cold and empty face and getting nothing back.

'It wasn't difficult to work out who was behind the murders. When I examined the bodies, I found all of them had a small spot of blood on their chests, right over their hearts.'

'But you said that couldn't have come from any kind of weapon you were familiar with,' said Diana.

'It wasn't a weapon, as such,' said Alistair. 'It was one of those long steel hairpins that June uses to hold her beehive hairdo in place. Remember, she showed you one earlier? Long and sharp enough to pierce the heart with a single thrust. All it left behind was a narrow wound that all but sealed itself.' He stopped and looked thoughtfully at June. 'I did wonder how you could be so sure about that. Would I be right in thinking you experimented on animals, to make sure it would work?'

June smiled suddenly. 'Every job has its fun parts. It turned out I needed to smear the pin with a special super-coagulant, to clot the blood and make sure it wouldn't give the game away. Who knew? Of course, I had to be really careful when I pushed it back into my hair.'

Alistair looked at her steadily. 'First you stabbed Indira, when you bent over her to wake her up. Then you did the same with Toby, when you got in close to confront him after the séance. And finally Leslie; after a completely out-of-character hug that got you close enough to do the deed, and hide what you were up to with your own body. Three people, dying live on camera, for no apparent reason. What else could be responsible . . . but the ghosts?'

Diana frowned. 'Why didn't she try to kill me, or you?'

'I'm pretty sure that was the plan,' said Alistair. 'But I was always so suspicious of her, she was having trouble getting close enough. And since I kept you close to me, you were safe too.'

'I knew there was a reason why I liked you so much,' said Diana.

'You had to be the killer, June,' said Alistair. 'Leslie just didn't have it in him to murder someone in cold blood. Though apparently he had no problem in setting people up, and then standing back and letting it happen.'

Diana glared at Leslie's body. 'Good riddance to bad rubbish.'

'June told us her technicians had been all over the hall in advance,' said Alistair. 'That was the first indication that the hall might not be everything it seemed, after they were through with it. Except . . . I don't believe there were any technicians, because June wouldn't have trusted them not to talk afterwards. She and Leslie must have done all the work themselves.'

'Would they have been able to?' said Diana. 'All this special-effects stuff sounds pretty complicated.'

'I can't imagine June having any part of her show that she didn't understand from top to bottom,' said Alistair. 'Just to make sure she'd always be in control. Remember how Leslie said June was always bullying her old technical crew, to get things right? She could do that because she knew their job as well as they did.'

Alistair nodded slowly to June. 'You and Leslie were excellent performers . . . Keeping us off balance with scary stories, and then pretending to see and hear things, while being so convincing we never doubted you for a moment. You acted like you believed, so we did too.'

'Of course!' said Diana. 'Remember the cold spots? They were so persuasive with their shakes and shudders that we felt cold ourselves!'

'Well,' said Alistair. 'Not all of us. If you remember, I did point out that their breath didn't steam on the air.'

'No one likes a show-off, darling,' said Diana. 'Get on with it.'

'They even kept up a series of carefully staged arguments,' said Alistair. 'Loudly disagreeing over whether or not there was a supernatural element to what was happening in the hall. Pre-empting any objection we might make, before it even occurred to us to do so. And lots of emotional fireworks going on between them, to hold the audience's attention; when the rest of us proved too easy-going, even after so much super-natural provocation.'

'I am genuinely embarrassed,' said Diana. 'An actress of my calibre, taken in so completely.'

'They were very good at it,' said Alistair. 'But then, they'd had a lot of practice at fooling people on all their previous shows.'

'What about the demon attack?' said Diana.

'There was no demon,' said Alistair. 'Leslie just acted so convincingly that we all believed him, and got swept up in the drama. That's why it ended so suddenly when I said a few useful words. Leslie needed a way out of the situation he'd created, before we started to notice the cracks in his story.'

Diana frowned. 'Then what about all those voices Leslie channelled, during the séance?'

'Careful research, a gift for mimicry, and tailoring his responses to the reactions he got,' said Alistair. 'He was a lot better at his job than you gave him credit for, June.'

He waited, but since there was still no response, he carried on. He tried to keep from rushing, even though he was getting to the end.

'I'm guessing the plan was for all four guests to die in mysterious circumstances, live on air; apparently scared to death in the most haunted hall in England. With only the two hosts surviving. That would put the show back on top again.'

'Of course,' said Diana. 'I can just see June and Leslie emerging from the hall after the time-locks opened, shocked and shaking and holding each other up, barely able to speak after the ordeal they'd been through . . . They could have milked that story for years. But would people really have believed them?'

'People have believed stranger things on reality television shows,' said Alistair.

'And the audience would have come back for more, week after week,' said Diana. 'Just in case it happened again.'

'You think you're so clever!' June said suddenly. As though she just couldn't stand to be silent any longer. Her calm professional face was gone, replaced by a cold, fuming rage. 'You were just as scared as everyone else!'

'Did I miss anything?' Alistair said politely.

June pulled a long steel pin from inside her beehive hairdo, and aimed it at Alistair and Diana like the weapon it was.

'Come anywhere near me, and I'll send you to join the others!'

Diana raised her fists. 'Do you really have the guts, to take on someone who's ready for you?'

June smiled. 'Try me, darling. It's not like I've anything left to lose. The only reason I'm not killing you both right now . . . is that I'm not dumb enough to take a risk I don't have to. Not when I can get out of here and disappear so completely that no one will ever find me.' She laughed breathily. 'I've had such a good time . . . Making you all jump like puppets while I pulled the strings. Watching your stupid faces as I fooled you all, again and again! Making you believe in things that weren't even there! Though, of course, that is what this show has always been about . . .'

'You needed Leslie's help to make it work,' said Alistair. 'How will you cope, without him?'

'Oh please!' said June. 'I carried that man! I had to lead him by the hand half the time tonight, feeding him cues for all the bits of business he was supposed to introduce. And he started the demon attack scenario far too early! That was supposed to come right at the end of the show, for the big climax! But it all worked out . . . Because we were so smart, and you were so gullible.

'And it was fun. Killing that insipid little Indira, and that seriously unfunny Toby. I should never have booked him. And, best of all, that complete waste of space, Leslie. I should have done it years ago, and replaced him with someone who knew what they were doing. You know, he really did believe he was an actual medium . . . Even though I made him show me all the tricks of his trade before I'd hire him.' She laughed again. 'Three dead, and they never saw me coming. I got to see their faces in their last moments, as they realized I was killing them. Ah . . . Memories to treasure. But now, it's time for me to move on. With all the money I took out of the show that the accountants never knew about.'

Diana started forward, but Alistair stopped her with a hand on her arm.

'Remember the stuff she smeared on the pin,' he said. 'Even a scratch might be dangerous.'

Diana growled under her breath, but stayed where she was.

'That's right,' said June. 'Be a sensible little over-the-hill actress, and don't try to follow me.'

'But where can you go?' said Alistair. 'Where could a public figure like you possibly hide out, where someone wouldn't recognize you?'

'June Colby isn't real,' said June. 'Just someone I created, because you need a dramatic host for a dramatic show.' She gestured at her Sixties outfit, and the towering beehive hairdo. 'You have no idea what I really look like, under all of this. No one does; that's the point. I'll just take it all off and become one of those ordinary everyday people that nobody ever notices, and lead a completely uninteresting life . . . Until it's time for me to reappear as someone else.'

'But how are you going to get out of the hall?' said Diana. 'The time-locks won't open for hours yet.'

'Oh please,' said June. 'You can't really believe I'd allow myself to be trapped in here? I have an override. The lock company presented it to me for free, because their insurance company insisted.'

She backed carefully away from Alistair and Diana, waving the steel pin back and forth to make sure they kept their distance. Diana stirred unhappily at Alistair's side, but his hand clamped down hard on her arm.

'We can't just let her get away!' Diana said urgently.

'She won't,' said Alistair.

'Tell me you have a plan,' said Diana.

'I have a plan.'

'Tell me it's a good plan.'

'I have a plan,' said Alistair.

He raised his voice, and adopted his most commanding tone. 'Stay where you are, June. You can't leave. The hall won't let you.'

And despite everything, June stopped and looked at him. Because even though she was right on the brink of making her escape, June was still concerned Alistair would find a way to stop her. He'd seen through her plans, uncovered what she'd done, and forced her to abandon her show, right on the edge of success. She wouldn't have stopped for threats, or appeals, but when he threw words at her that made no sense . . . She had to stop, and see what he was doing.

'You're only alive because I couldn't be bothered to kill you,' said June. 'Make yourselves a problem, and I will find the time to deal with you.'

'You can't,' Alistair said calmly. 'We're protected.'

'What?' said June.

'Yes,' Diana said quietly. 'What she said. Where is this going, Alistair?'

'Hush,' he said to her, just as quietly. 'I'm putting ideas in her head. Watch for your cues, and play along.' He raised his voice again, holding June's gaze with his own. He filled his voice with authority, and his face with certainty. 'After everything that's happened here, June, are you sure you don't believe in the supernatural? In the presence that haunts this hall? All kinds of things have been happening that had nothing to do with you and your plans. Leslie understood. He kept trying to tell you we were not alone here, that there was something in this place that you and he hadn't allowed for. Something beyond your control.'

'I'm always in control!' said June. 'I had a script for my show all along; you just never knew it was a murder mystery.'

'If you'd been able to follow your script,' said Alistair, 'Diana and I would have been dead long before this.'

'Don't give her ideas,' Diana murmured.

Alistair concentrated all his attention on June. She might not want to believe what he was saying, but she couldn't stop listening.

'Leslie was always more open than you,' said Alistair. 'He could see that there were things out of place. He was the first to feel a presence that didn't belong. You never had any faith in his abilities, but he did. He tried to warn you, but you wouldn't listen. You invaded this hall, altered its structure to suit your own purposes, and made it your killing ground. You woke something up. Do you really think it will let you leave?'

'I don't believe in the supernatural!' said June.

'It doesn't care whether you believe,' said Alistair. 'It's not a ghost, or a demon; it's a *genius loci*. The spirit of the place. Born of a town's fears and needs, content to lurk in the background; until you disturbed it.' He stopped, and looked around him. 'It's here . . . I can feel it, watching us.'

'Unseen eyes,' said Diana, peering quickly around her. 'That's what the townspeople said. I can feel it too, and it's getting closer.'

'Stop it!' said June. 'I don't believe you!'

But she wouldn't have sounded so upset if that had been true.

'You can't hide from it,' said Alistair. 'You can't escape, because it won't let you. Not after everything you've done. It wants to make you pay, to keep you here, imprisoned and suffering; for ever.'

June's head swivelled quickly back and forth as she glared around the hall. Her face was strained, and beaded with sweat. Alistair had created a persuasive atmosphere with his words and, despite everything, June was starting to believe.

An overhead tube light flickered, and went out. Followed by another. Diana cried out, and huddled up against Alistair. June fell back a step, and then made herself stop. She pulled a remote control out of a hidden pocket in her outfit and frantically worked the controls, but the lights didn't come back on. June shook the control hard, and tried again, but the lights weren't answering her.

'Work!' she said loudly. 'Why won't you work?'

'You know why,' said Alistair. 'All your tricks can't protect you now.'

June threw the control at him, and it skidded along the floor. 'What have you done?'

'Not me,' said Alistair. 'This is all down to you, June. You brought this on yourself. But it's not too late. Drop the weapon and surrender yourself to me, and I will get you out of here safely. Under my protection.'

'Surrender to you?' said June. 'Never.'

She charged straight at him, holding the pin out before her. Alistair couldn't look away. He had to trust Diana to have faith in him, and hold her ground. And of course she did. Alistair waited till June was almost on top of him, and then he scooped up one of the sleeping bags from the floor and threw it over her. The heavy folds enveloped June, and she stumbled to a halt, thrashing blindly about her. Diana grabbed up the remote-control box from the floor, and brought it slamming down on June's head. There was a heavy thud, and June collapsed. She fell forward, still wrapped in the sleeping bag. She convulsed briefly on the floor, and then lay still. Alistair and Diana watched her for a while.

'She's not moving,' said Diana. 'I didn't think I hit her that hard.' She looked at the remote control in her hand, and threw it away.

'I don't think this was down to you,' said Alistair.

He knelt beside the shrouded form, and pulled carefully at the folds of the sleeping bag.

'Careful!' said Diana. 'It could be another of her tricks.'

'I don't think so,' said Alistair.

He eased back enough of the bag to reveal June's face. Her eyes stared sightlessly. He put a hand to her neck, but there was no trace of a pulse. He shook his head.

'She's gone.'

'She's dead?' said Diana. 'How did that happen? I didn't hit her that hard!' A thought came to her, and she looked around her. 'Did the hall kill her?'

'I don't think so,' said Alistair.

He pulled away more of the sleeping bag and rolled June on to her side. The steel hairpin protruded from June's chest.

'She fell on her own weapon . . .' said Diana.

'Hoist on her own petard,' said Alistair.

He got to his feet, and Diana hugged him fiercely.

'Well done, Bish. You really got to her. Did you believe any
of the stuff you were saying?'

'Of course not. I was just trying to mess with her head
enough that she would surrender. Well done, though, for
picking up on my cues once you saw where I was going.'

'I am an actress, darling,' said Diana.

She let go of him, and they both looked at the body on the
floor.

'I never wanted her to die,' said Alistair.

'Yes, well, that's you,' said Diana. 'I feel a lot safer now.'
She looked round the hall. 'And just maybe . . . Something
here wanted her dead. Why did those lights go out when they
did?'

'Outdated wiring,' said Alistair.

Diana looked at him. 'You really believe that?'

'I will if you will,' said Alistair. 'Let's get the hell out of
here.'

He knelt down again, searched June carefully, and found a
small steel box with a single red button on it.

'Always keep it simple, for the technologically challenged,'
said Alistair.

He pointed the box at the main doors and hit the button,
and the time-locks sprang open. Alistair offered Diana his arm,
and she slipped her arm through his. Alistair looked back at
the cameras on the walls.

'Good night, folks. Hope you enjoyed the show.'

He led Diana over to the doors, and she snuggled up against
him.

'We're going to have some story to tell. The things it will
do for my career! And yours too, of course.'

'We may have to wait, to find someone to tell it to,' said
Alistair. 'I don't think there's anybody out there.'

'What do you mean?' said Diana. 'June told the director to
contact the police and the rescue services.'

'I don't believe there ever was a director,' said Alistair. 'Or
a crew in a trailer in the car park. I had a good look round
when I arrived, and I didn't see a trailer anywhere. Can you
really see June allowing anyone else to have control over her
show? No; I think everything that happened here went out

live, entirely uninterrupted. Because her ego wouldn't allow anything less. It wasn't enough that she had planned the perfect murders; the whole world had to see it happen.' He shook his head slowly. 'As if the twenty-seven people who died here weren't enough.'

'Surely the police will turn up at some point?' said Diana.

'Eventually,' said Alistair. 'We're in a small country town, far from anywhere. And what a tale we'll have to tell them.'

Diana looked at him steadily. 'Was anything here real?'

'Just the cameras,' said Alistair.

'Then let's give the audience one last thrill,' said Diana.

She threw her arms around Alistair, and kissed him. And because she was an actress, she made a real production out of it. Alistair did his best to keep up. They finally separated, and grinned at each other.

'Two stars are born!' Alistair said grandly.

'Of course!' said Diana. 'The Actress and the Bishop!'

'The Holy Terrors!' said Alistair.

Laughing together, they walked out of the hall.